All I Wank for Christmas

TORI ROSS

This book is dedicated to Nathan F.

He's not my husband, brother, or cousin. In fact, I haven't seen him in over 30 years. He's the little douche canoe that told me Santa wasn't real when we were in first grade.

Fuck you, Nathan.

Author's Note

If you read the dedication page, you know how I learned the truth about Santa when I was in first grade. Part of why that random classmate was able to convince me Santa isn't real right there on our Lutheran school playground was because I already had questions.

Question #1- How the fuck is Santa able to deliver to every single child in the world? Even at six, I was worldly enough to know what a large-scale job that is.

Question #2- How can he get into houses if he doesn't have a chimney?

As you read this book, you'll have similar questions, even if you're a grown ass adult and already playing Santa to your own children. The truth is, there's just no way to write a realistic Santa book, but I've attempted to answer some of these questions, partly because I don't want all the reviews about a Santa book that will inevitably say, "Totally made up." Let's just get that out of the way right now – I totally made up my own rules about how Santa gets the job done.

So, kick back and relax. This book isn't something to take seriously. Nothing would make me happier than to know it took one of my readers away from our shitshow reality for a few hours.

It's magic. Christmas magic...because there really isn't any better type of magic.

Let's do this. Buckle up.

Contents

Chapter 1

HOLLY

I give amazing hand jobs. It's a gift.

Not everyone can do it well. Most hand job givers are either unenthusiastic or too eager to please. It's a fine line to walk and get it right. It's a blessing and a curse to be good at it, but I've been thankful for my handy gift every single day since Grant McHammond taught me how to slide all the way up the shaft and follow through up the head during orientation week at Illinois State. He was also the first to teach me that ball play is fair play. Cupping. Massaging. Even a clockwise nuzzle over the ole taint spot with my index finger is all part of the hand job experience. I quickly became known as Holly Happy Hands Hepperdine around my college campus.

I'm especially thankful for my ability now that it's my family's livelihood.

Sure, I have a degree in accounting. I *may* be a certified public accountant. Fat lot of fucking good it's done me in this small town in the hills of Pennsylvania where nothing happens and corporate jobs are scarce. I had to come back home when Mom fell sick with an autoimmune disorder. Dad did the typical "going out for milk" runner about ten years ago. It's been hard, but I'll be God damned if my younger sister, Helena, has to quit community college because of lack of tuition.

Someone has to pay the bills, pay Helena's tuition, and take care of Mom until the social security office wants to process that disability claim. That same someone also can't find a remote accounting job to save her life. I guess companies don't want to gamble on remote workers that just graduated. Maybe they want people to show up to the office the first few years as an accountant to prove themselves. I blame generation bias.

Whatever the reason, I'm back in my childhood town working at the Happy Stroke Club. The club was the only place hiring. My town is too small for a Target or a Walmart. My only other choices were the Chinese restaurant that only hires family members and the rest area by the interstate.

Something tells me I made the safe choice of not working at the rest area. I'd rather give hand jobs in a climate-controlled facility than work a glory hole.

I work in a small massage parlor that you practically need special directions to find. It's a small brick building with a faded sign and a gravel parking lot. Most clients park around back because the back of the building backs up to the woods. We picked a rural area so clients' wives wouldn't drive by on their way to the grocery store and see their husbands' cars in the lot. It's sad as fuck, but it's worked well for the owner, Linda One.

Don't feel sorry for me, though. Tips are good. I never have to use a calculator. I don't have to stock shelves. Or mop.

Well, I do have to mop. Sometimes things get…messy. That's the only drawback of this job, though. I get the job satisfaction of hearing a man who hasn't been laid in a year moan like an animal as I cup my gloved hand over his dick and catch his load in my hand, often cooing over such a beautiful orgasm. They like it when you compliment the release arc as it moves through the air. After all, if you want good tips at a hand job joint you have to make the men feel like they are the brightest star of your day and their orgasm is exciting and original.

Then again, I think that's all men.

"Holly!" Linda One yells from the front of the shop, causing me to jump. "Client here to see you."

I don't think her name is really Linda. If you go into a massage parlor and every woman in the joint is named Linda, that's your first sign it's one of *those* massage places. At a rub and tug, we're *all* Lindas. I'm not sure why I use my real name with most clients. Probably because I grew up here, and the town won't buy the Linda bullshit with me. It's awkward to give a fake name to your old high school math teacher when you're massaging his balls.

Most men know this Linda tip, and I feel sorry for legitimate masseuses named Linda.

Other signs you're in one of *those* massage parlors? A fake flower, usually a rose, is on the table in the massage room, the place only accepts cash, and they're open late into the evening, sometimes twenty-four hours.

Legitimate massage places often deal with men asking to be finished, and it's a good way to be banned from the premises. You never ask to be finished if you're in a legitimate joint. If you're unsure, the rule of thumb should always be to wait for your massage personnel to ask if you want a "full release."

If you're wanting your gherkin jerked, you're in the right place at The Happy Stroke Club. Full release is on the menu board above the desk. Sometimes, I'm not sure how we've flown under the law enforcement radar.

Actually, I do know. Sheriff DeWitt, the head poohbah of the county police, and his department come in every Thursday afternoon for "team building." I guess team building includes separate jerk-off sessions with the ladies here and not trust falls or beer over happy hour. We're their "happy" hour plan. They keep the feds and the state troopers away for selfish reasons.

I take a deep breath and roll my shoulders, walking to the front of the shop where Linda One smiles at an older man from behind the counter. His hair is white and combed to the side like Donald Trump's hairstylist did his hair this morning, and he wears glasses with gold frames.

Another man, a younger one, flips through a magazine on the chair in the corner of the waiting room. I do a double take when I come into the room. I'm used to the older guys. I'm not used to a drop-dead gorgeous guy with dark tousled hair, beard stubble, and shoulders like a brick shit house that could get any woman he wants.

He's not from around here, and he smiles as he puts down the magazine he's holding, blinks twice, and tilts his head to the side as he runs his eyes over me.

Fuck me.

"Holly!" Linda snaps, causing me to startle again. "This client has a gift card he got a few days early." She points to the older man and then gestures to the Christmas special display where clients can buy gift cards for their friends. "This man says he needs extra help."

They all say that.

"Of course," I say, tearing my eyes away from the hot piece of ass in the corner and extending my hand to the older man. I try not to slouch in disappointment with the knowledge I'll spend too much time with the older guy, and my coworker, Linda Two, will get to yank the stud. "I'm Holly. I'll be your service provider today. Come on back."

I glance one last time at the younger man, and his eyes follow me as I leave the room. He squints and frowns, and it's obvious he's sad I won't be his jerker today. If I didn't know better, I'd say his face is lined with concern. I half expect him to follow me to make sure I'm safe.

I lead the older man into my room, and he grunts as he climbs on the table without even looking around. Most men want to look at every single thing when they get back here for the first time. I guess they think there will be toys, whips, chains, or something scandalous.

I run my eyes over the walls, bare except for a few pictures Linda One got from a garage sale. I have a white counter that holds clean sheets for the table, gloves, and cleaner. It looks like the standard doctor's office counter with a small sink attached in case I need water for an especially messy client. Otherwise, the sheet-covered massage table in the room is the only clue of what goes on here.

"What kind of services do you do to help?" the man asks, clasping his hands over his stomach and staring at the ceiling. "I'm desperate. My wife has given up all hope."

One of *those* guys. I see a lot of the guys that use a little blue pill. Either that, or they need a twenty-four-year-old woman in high heels and a short skirt to get hard. That's where I come in.

"I'll fix you right as rain, sir," I say, propping a pillow under his knees. "It was nice of your friend to give you a gift card for my services."

"My wife bought it for me."

Huh. That's a little unorthodox. Most wives don't want their husbands coming here. Maybe his wife likes the idea of him fucking around with someone else and then coming home to her and telling her about it? I get that once or twice a month. One client likes to record the session and stream it to his wife.

Whatever. I don't kink shame.

"Where would you like me to focus?"

He waves his hands over his torso and down to his thighs. "On the problem."

"Of course."

I snap on some gloves, and he eyes me warily. "Is that necessary?" he asks.

"Oh, yes. Things can get messy, and we are safe and sanitary at The Happy Stroke Club."

"Well, I guess that's fine," he says, chewing on his lip. "Will this hurt?"

What kind of sadist has been handling his skin flute? This man clearly needs me, and I should have his wife come in for a lesson or something. "No, sir. I think you'll find the treatment most pleasant."

He relaxes and closes his eyes, and I wonder if I should have him take his glasses off. Some guys are shooters and get it all over.

I unbutton my blouse until my cleavage shows. This increases tips, especially if they ask to palm my breasts while I finish them. The men feel like they owe me something extra then, and I've never had a problem with it. Nothing wrong with a little afternoon nipple flick.

"You can touch me if you like," I whisper, massaging up the man's legs on my way to his fly.

"Why would I touch you? I'm the one getting stroke care."

"Fair enough," I say. I move my hands from his knees and up his thighs.

When I get to his pants and start to unbutton them, he gasps and rolls to his side. He swipes my hands away and looks at me like I've hurt him. I instinctually step back, and my butt hits the counter behind me.

"What the hell are you doing, young lady? Are you trying to touch my pecker? What does this have to do with stroke care?"

Oh shit. The pieces come together like the last few missing pieces of a puzzle. This happens now and then, so it's not a new situation, but I take my gloves off with a snap and throw them in the nearby metal can.

He looks at me with a look of revulsion and horror. "I don't understand," he mumbles.

"What did your wife tell you when she gave you the gift card?"

He squints and looks at the ceiling like he's trying to remember. "Well, she said that she found a new place specializing in strokes. She thought it would help me since I had my stroke this past spring."

I sigh and put my hands on my hips. I force my lips into a straight line. I don't dare smile or laugh when this happens because that's a sure way to set them off. "I'm sure The Happy Stroke Club name would be something a woman without knowledge of rub and tugs would think is a rehabilitation facility for stroke victims."

"It's not? What kind of place is this?" he asks, swinging his legs off the table and still looking at me with wide eyes.

"It's the other kind of stroke club." He looks at me blankly, and I pinch my nose. Some innocent folks are slower on the uptake. "Sir, we stroke dicks here."

His mouth drops open and he looks around the room as if noticing that he's in a massage parlor for the first time. He eyes the bottle of cleaner on the table and the box of rubber gloves by the sink. Slowly, he slinks off the table and looks back at it with a grimace, probably wondering if he should go home and wash his pants.

I keep my room as clean as possible, but he should probably run the pants through the hot cycle.

His hands shake, and I'm mildly worried he'll have another stroke on my floor. I pat his arm. "Let me take you back up front and Linda One will refund the money for your wife's gift card."

A gurgling sound comes from his mouth like he's finding words to say or just trying to catch his breath. He lets me lead him to the lobby, and he looks around the hallway like he's seeing it for the first time.

When I get to the lobby, the hot guy is still sitting in the chair waiting for Linda Two. Maybe she's on lunch. Maybe he's waiting for Linda Three. Whatever the case, he's still there, and he smiles when I walk into the room. "It's you!" he says with a smile, dropping the magazine again.

I hand off the older gentleman to Linda One and mouth, "Stroke victim." She sighs and waves the man over to the counter for a refund. I don't think the man has blinked since I tried to touch his cock.

Walking to the gorgeous man, I tilt my head and smile. "Do I know you?" I ask.

"Nope," the man replies with a little shake of his head. His eyes light up like a spotlight, and he gives me another look up and down my body. He clears his throat and focuses on my face. Only then do I remember my shirt is still unbuttoned enough for my C-cup breasts to pop out.

"Oh, I just thought maybe we knew each other since you seemed to know me just now."

He shrugs. "I just saw you a few minutes ago. I was hoping you'd be my masseuse, but you went back with that guy. I guess I was disappointed when you left and felt happy when you came back."

What. A. Cinnamon. Roll.

"That's sweet. Did a Linda come and get you yet, or are you waiting for a specific masseuse?"

"I think I'd like you if that's alright."

My heart drops to the floor. I only get to jerk off guys this hot when I have an actual Tinder date and choose them myself. Gorgeous men who look like they could model on the cover of *GQ* don't exactly rush into a small-town rub and tug. Maybe he's someone's bored relative who has nothing better to do in our town over Christmas and is only surrounded by cousins who would be unsuitable for hand jobs.

"Have you recently suffered a stroke?" I ask, not wanting to have a repeat of the last man.

"No." He furrows his brow and frowns. "Does that matter?"

"Nope. Just checking. Come on back," I say, turning and waving for him to follow me. "Welcome to The Happy Stroke Club."

I don't expect him to tell me his name. None of the men do. Sure, I know the police department, my math teacher, my old gym teacher, the deacon at my childhood church, and the guy that runs the fish fry. But they don't say their names, and I don't say them during the procedure. It gets weird. It's probably like the town gynecologist pretending they've never looked inside your vagina or given you a breast exam when they run into you at Taco Bell. What I do is a business transaction, end of story.

It catches me off guard when I hear a husky whisper behind me. "I'm Jasper."

Chapter 2

JASPER

From the moment she walked into the waiting room, I wanted to talk to her. The idea of her massaging my back is nice, but I want to *know* her. Learn her name. I want to know where she buys those cute red and white striped tights she's wearing under the flouncy red skirt with what looks like garland around the hem. I want to know why she chose bangs over letting her thick, dark hair fly freely around her face. What's her favorite color? Does she cheer for the Phillies, or is she a Pirates fan? Most importantly, Eagles or Steelers?

I run my eyes down the back of her as she silently leads me into her massage room. She's very fit. Probably a runner by the judge of her calves. I smile, thinking of her out on a morning run, her hair back in a ponytail that flops when she jogs. I try not to think about her in tight running shorts and a white sports bra with her nipples...

"Here we are," she says, gesturing toward the massage table in the middle of the room.

I look around at the walls. Hmm. Most massage places have relaxing pictures on the walls or soft music piped through the speakers. Maybe some incense or a pot of potpourri. This is different. Functional. The only pictures on the walls don't match. There's a framed cat stuck in a boot on one side of the room and a guy with a fishing pole on the opposite wall.

I pick up a paper rose at the foot of the table and sniff it. I don't know why. I just wanted to see if it smelled nice or smells like her own perfume. Disappointed when I smell nothing but the faint hint of cleaner, I drop the paper flower and wish I had the foresight to buy her real flowers.

I never thought I'd meet someone so beautiful with a smile that lights up the room. She's certainly not what I expected to find in a ramshackle building that needs serious brick updates and a new roof.

"Well, go ahead and get comfortable," she says, clapping her hands and raising her eyebrows.

Her eyes widen and darken into black holes as she takes me in, studying me from my forehead to the tips of my boots. I hope I look normal. Be normal. Just for a few minutes. I only need this beautiful woman to give me a massage that will relieve all this family stress and delivery pressure of tonight. I have a lot on my plate. None of this needs to be weird.

"Don't you leave while I get undressed? Is there a robe I can use?"

She shrugs. "If you want," she says. Fuck, her voice is like soft butter. "Most clients don't see the point since I'm going to see their junk anyway. We don't exactly fuss with privacy, but I'm happy to give you a moment."

"Their junk?"

She blows out a deep breath and crosses her arms over her chest. "I thought you said you weren't here because you had a stroke."

I shake my head, not understanding. "I haven't."

"Are you here because your friends dared you to check in, grab my boob, and then run out?"

"People do that?" I ask.

"It happens more often than I'd like to admit. We have some fraternities a few towns over, and I'd hate to be one of their pledges."

"That seems a tad disrespectful."

"You know that we're a rub and tug, right?" she asks.

I tilt my head to the side, smiling. "What's that? Is that a special kind of massage?"

"I don't know why I don't just wear a sandwich sign over my torso." She bites her lip and looks away from me. I want her eyes back on mine. I don't like it when she looks away. "My job is to jerk you off." She enunciates the words, and it takes a second for me to understand.

I spin around in a circle, hands on hips like I'm looking at an old house I'm going to purchase. "This isn't a regular massage place?"

"No. You're in a special massage facility. We only massage dicks here."

The penny drops and things make sense. Her unbuttoned blouse. The women only named Linda. All the cars around back but none in the front lot. I didn't see any female clients in the waiting area.

She taps her foot and looks at the floor. "If you want to go, I'll have Linda One refund your money. There seems to be a rash of misunderstandings today."

No! I can't leave. I like her. I want her hands on me. So what if I thought I was going to get the stress massaged from my shoulders. If she wants to massage that stress straight out of my dick, that's even better, right? I can't leave now. I won't get to talk to her. I won't find out her favorite color.

I silently get on the table and squeeze my eyes shut. "I've never done this before."

"You don't say?" she laughs. "I thought it was a little weird that you were here."

I open one eye to find her pulling purple rubber gloves over her hands. My dentist uses something similar. "Why is it weird?"

She laughs and covers her mouth with her forearm like she's trying to hide it. "You're not our usual clientele. We get older men and a lot of younger men without girlfriends or wives for whatever reason. You don't strike me as someone who has a problem getting a girlfriend or even getting someone to give you a hand job."

This is news to me. I can't get a girlfriend to save my life, especially not where I live. There's not exactly a lot of selection in rural Canada. If I travel for a date, the woman usually doesn't like me or the date is terrible. How would I even explain my family and my job to a woman? I'd sound like a lunatic. It's probably my fault that I shut down on dates, not wanting to give away too much information.

Now that I'm relaxed and on a massage table with a moment to think about it, I probably come across as a serial killer on dates. Their radar goes up as soon as I hem and haw over details of my life. Hell, I can't even come up with believable hobbies when they ask what I do in my spare time. What am I going to say? Would any woman believe I help train reindeer?

"No girlfriend," I whisper as the woman's hands hover near the drawstring of my pants.

She frowns and pats my chest. "Are you comfortable with me undoing your pants or would you like to do it?"

The idea of her fingers untying the drawstring, even if they're gloved in latex, makes me harden. I can't remember the last time I've been touched by a woman. Months? Years? How did I let it go that long?

I know how it happened. Dad got sick. I had to take over most of the operation except for the yearly big night delivery. This is my first year taking care of that, hence the stress. Unfortunately, our family business isn't conducive to getting hot babes to give you a hand job.

I clear my throat. "I'd like you to do everything that's allowed, now that I know what's involved here."

"The works, huh?" She smiles, and I could stare at it all night. Her teeth are perfectly white and straight except for one of her front teeth that tilts slightly to the side, causing a small gap that's unnoticeable unless you're looking.

And I *really* can't stop looking at her.

Where did she come from? How did this beautiful creature that could be a model or movie star end up giving hand jobs to old men in the middle of bumfuck Pennsylvania?

"Would you like music?" she asks, pulling me out of my thoughts of whisking her away and buying her the condo she deserves somewhere near a beach.

"Uh, do other clients do music?"

She smiles and looks at the ceiling like she's thinking. "Actually, only the former band teacher ever asked for music. That's odd, huh?"

"Not if he loves music." I smile a ridiculous smile, hoping to see her smile again. Fuck, I want to make her laugh. "Do you get a lot of people you know?"

"I'm not supposed to say. Everything is confidential." Her voice is so relaxing, I don't even notice that my pants are already undone.

She gestures for me to lift my butt so she can pull my waistband down. I try to remember what underwear I wore today and blow out a sigh of relief when I see the simple, red boxer briefs. Thank fuck it wasn't the ones with elves and the countdown to Christmas my mother likes to put in my drawer as a joke around this time of year.

"You don't have to give names," I say.

"True. I get some surprises. Let's just say I've jerked my fair share of former teachers, police officers, firemen, and my coworkers and I each did our share of a bus full of Baptist ministers passing through on their way to a revival last year. That was exhausting and painful the next day. Good tips, though." She smiles at the memory, and I can't help but chuckle at the idea of a bus letting ministers off in the parking lot.

"It's funny who we *don't* get," she says, keeping her eyes on the ceiling like she's waiting for me to be comfortable with the situation.

"Who don't you get?" I ask. This is fucking fascinating.

She laughs and bites her lips as she slips my underwear down. She doesn't look at my dick yet as it bobs below my belly button, fully erect and weeping for her to touch me. The urge to touch myself while I look at her face burns up and down my body, and I flex my fingers. She doesn't even need to touch me today. I'd enjoy running my fingers through her hair and looking at her while I take care of myself.

"You know the guys that everyone thinks would come here? Guys with motorcycles, tattoos, and beards? The guys that hang out at pool halls and drink lots of beer?"

"Yeah," I drawl.

"I don't see them. Ever. It's like they don't exist in here. But I can tell you which married alderman has a mole on his left testicle."

I laugh, and she laughs with me. I'd even classify it as a giggle. It hasn't just been a long time since someone has touched my dick. It's been forever since a woman has laughed at something I said or did. A real laugh. Not one of those fake chuckles someone does when they think they're supposed to laugh.

She glances at my dick, and I flinch. What if she hates it? What if it doesn't compare to the other dicks she sees on a daily basis?

Her tongue darts out so fast that I almost miss it as it wets her lips. Her eyes widen for a moment before she shakes her head and blinks. I almost come when she simply presses her right hand on my stomach. "This is quite the beautiful dick you have, Jasper."

"You probably say that to all the guys."

She tilts her head and hums. "There are fake compliments to get tips, and there are dicks you'd work for free."

"Can I get my money back then?" I ask.

"No."

"Worth a shot."

She reaches for a bottle of lube on the counter, flips open the cap, and squeezes a small drop at the top of my dick and on the underside of my cock at the base. "Will that be enough?" I ask.

"To start," she says. "But you're so sweet, I thought I'd give you a little extra."

Extra what?

She dips her head, and I squeeze the table. Is she going to put her mouth on me? I didn't realize a blow job was an option, but I did just ask for the full works. I'm not mentally prepared for a blow job from this woman. I'll come too fast. I'll explode in her mouth, and she'll laugh at me with the other Lindas. I'll be unmanned!

She hovers over my cock for a moment, turns her head, looks into my eyes, and drops a line of spit onto the head of my dick. It's the hand on my stomach that is the keeper, though. It's warm and intimate, even with the latex between us. She wants to bring me pleasure, but she wants to touch me somewhere else while she does it.

I practically swoon from the warm spit as it drips down the underside of my dick, and my eyes flutter as she smiles an evil grin. Her left hand grips the base of my cock, and she drags the lube from the base until it meets her spit at the head, mixing to make warm, slippery lubrication.

"Feel good?" she whispers.

Naughty list. This woman has to be somewhere on the naughty list. No nice girl could do what she's doing to my dick. Most women keep their hands in the same place when they jerk a dick. They just tug. This glorious angel of all hand jobs drags her hand from base to head and even throws in the elusive wrist twist. When I start to lose lubrication, she bends down and spits down my dick again in such an unladylike manner that tears form in my eyes at the beauty of a glob of drool teetering on my dick hole.

"Fuck," I moan.

"I'll take that as a yes. Let me know if you want different pressure."

She switches hands, and I miss the hand on my stomach. Only after it's gone do I realize it was the only thing keeping my back from arching off the table as she works me. I clench my abdomen to stay in place. It would be ungentlemanly to buck into her hand like I've never been touched.

But she's touching me like I've never been touched before. She knows moves I've never tried on myself.

She jerks my dick but moves her free hand to my balls, where she cups them perfectly like she's holding a baby bird that's fallen from the nest. Firm to hold them. Gentle to not crush them.

When she gives them a soft squeeze and moves her middle finger to the piece of skin just above my asshole, I lose all sense of composure. There is no chivalry. There is no pretending this isn't glorious. I clench my ass as I rise off the table. I bite my lip until I taste the metallic tang of blood.

This woman is a goddess. She's a holy disciple of hand jobs sent straight from heaven.

She rubs my taint spot in a clockwise motion with her firm middle finger while pressing her warm palm against my balls, moving them with a slow clockwise motion. Bending down, she drools on my cock again, and the combined feel of the wet spit, the ball fluff, and the dick tug sets my body on fire.

My toes curl. My toned legs shake. I temporarily forget who I am and the stress that caused me to stop here before the night's run. There's no thought in my head but how her hands feel on my entire manhood region.

I'm utterly fucked.

I'm clay to be molded in her hands.

I'm definitely coming back every chance I get and getting a gift card for myself so I have something tangible to pull out of my wallet and hold while I think of her.

My mouth opens in a silent moan, and I'm pretty sure my eyes roll back in my head. Reaching out, I feel for her. Anything. Hair. Cheek. Clavicle. Big toe. I reach for anything she'll let me touch. Her hand comes off my dick for a split second as she presses her breast into my hand. I force my eyes open and see her pink nipple exposed and pulled out of her shirt.

"You can touch me, Jasper. I miss being touched by someone too."

I palm her breast as she works me over, and I curl up a little like I'm doing a sit-up, intent on watching her work me. My eyes flutter, but I force them open. I need to see the breast I'm holding. I can feel her nipple hardening in my palm, but I want to commit it to memory. I *need* to watch her nipple tighten and harden when I flick it. I want to watch her slide her hand up and down my cock.

This hand job is a Christmas miracle the likes of which haven't been seen by humanity since a star guided shepherds and a boy played a drum for some barn animals.

I swipe her shirt aside and hold a crunch like I haven't had to do since eighth-grade gym class. She gasps when I palm both breasts, massaging and pinching her nipples as I buck into her hand without shame. Her gorgeous, almond-shaped eyes find my own, and we stare at each other while I pump into her hand like a deranged maniac. I watch her long lashes as she blinks as if in slow motion. Rays of sunlight surround her head.

I know I'm imagining the halo since we're in a windowless room, but someone should build a shrine to this woman's palm.

The moan comes out of my mouth before the cum sprays into her cupped hand above my dick. She knows exactly when to move the hand from my balls, and she knows to keep jerking my dick until every drop is drained from my body. Most men never have the patience to teach a woman to do it this way. They sure can't articulate it when someone's touching them.

I shake. I may curse a little, but I can't be sure what I'm saying. If I only knew her name.

I *have* to know her name. If nothing else, I need to know what name I'm going to moan when I jerk myself off for the next five years.

"There we go. All stress gone," she coos. "Feel better?"

"Am I dead? Is this heaven?"

She laughs and pulls her gloves off. She hands me a paper towel, and I look around for what she wants me to wipe. I'm not wet. I even look at my softening dick to see if drops dribbled around my manscaped bush. Nothing.

She waves in the direction of my knees, and I take the hint, pulling up my pants. I wiggle my legs to make the muscles work so I can swing my legs off the table.

Wait. Should I get her off? I'm sure most of her clients don't touch her clit, but I want to make her shatter around me. My mouth waters for her. Should I offer? Gesture for her to pull her panties down her beautiful legs? Damn, I'd eat her pussy until she cried. I want to run my stubble up her thighs and know what kind of noise she makes when *she* comes.

"Thanks for brightening my day, Jasper."

I startle a little and shake my head. Why is she thanking *me*? "I think that was the other way around."

"You were different. I don't say this to every client, but I enjoyed making you happy. Did you get a punch card when you came in?"

I frown. "There's a punch card? You have punch cards for hand jobs?"

"Of course. Ten regular price jerk offs, and the eleventh one is free. Not including tip, that is. Most places like this have them." We stare at each other in silence. "For the truckers."

"Ah! Yes, the truckers," I say, standing up and patting my pants pockets.

Wallet. Keys. There's nothing to do but leave. She's holding a bottle of cleaner to spray down the table and getting a new, white sheet out of the cabinet below the sink. I feel like I'm at a restaurant and the waitress is rushing me out to turn over the table.

It's now or never. "Will you tell me your name, or is that not allowed? Are you also a Linda?"

She straightens from where she was getting a clean sheet. "Not a Linda. I'll tell you my name, though. Most of the people in town know it anyway, so I don't see the big deal." She shrugs and holds out her hand for me to shake. "I'm Holly."

Holly... Holly... Rural Pennsylvania. Messina County. I run through the mental list of everyone named Holly in this area, mentally matching the name with people around her age. It's easy enough when I briefly close my eyes and focus. I've had the gift of recalling names and whether someone is a good person since I was born.

I'm my father's son and heir, after all.

Holly...

Naughty list in 2005 for continuously pinching her sister that summer and telling her mother the marks were mosquito bites. Nice list all other years of childhood, except for the year when she rode the line after a small incident with locking her grandfather in his lawn shed when he wouldn't buy her an ice cream cone. Dad is always lenient when it's that close, so she avoided coal that year. Naughty list in 2017 for...my face reddens at the thought. They called her Holly Happy Hands Hepperdine that year.

Hepperdine. Holly Hepperdine.

I need to pull myself together and not let on that I know all this. I certainly can't let on that I know her last name since she didn't tell me. I'd sound like a crazy stalker.

I dig into my sweatshirt pocket and pull out the twenty-dollar bill I was prepared to use as a tip for a normal massage. She definitely earned it, even if I feel dirty giving it to her. I wish I could give her more, but unless leaving her my credit card is an option, this is what I have. Hell, I wish I could give her anything she wants and mentally weigh the cons of actually leaving the credit card and telling her to buy herself something pretty.

I hold out the tip money, and she takes it, smiling a small smile without teeth and nodding. At the last minute, I remember I *can* give her something else.

"Here," I say, also holding out one of the candy canes that are always in my sweatshirt pocket. It's wrapped in green ribbon, and she eyes it like she's never seen a candy cane before taking it. "Merry Christmas, Holly."

Chapter 3

HOLLY

"I'm glad you had a good day, Mom," I say, tucking my mother into a burrito-like cocoon with blankets that are as old as Helena.

If I ever make enough money, I'm getting my mother all new blankets. And socks. She never buys socks for herself, choosing to patch or darn the old ones. Any money she got for clothes or bedding went into new school stuff for me or Helena every year. What she had left, she used on thrift shop finds for herself.

Some people wish they could get rich and buy their parents a new house. I'd buy my mother socks, blankets, *and* a new house. I'd buy her a healthy body if I could afford it.

It's cold in here. The heat is low because it's expensive and I give hand jobs for a living. It keeps food on the table and pants on our butts, but it won't hurt us to wear sweaters and bundle up in extra blankets to save on heat. I try to cut costs where I can.

"Are we opening gifts tomorrow?" Mom asks. Her face looks so much older than her fifty-eight years now. The disease is hitting her hard, and I blink back the tears at her child-like excitement for unwrapping gifts. She doesn't get much excitement now that she can't go to her cards club or even work a regular office job. There are no nights out for drinks with coworkers or book club meetings for her. She can't even go to church easily and requires Helena and me to help her in and out of the car and building. Funny that men stand in the parking lot and watch us struggle to lift her into her chair without lifting a finger. Maybe they don't want to get too close to the woman that gives them their hand jobs behind their wives' backs. So much for compassion. Since Helena works most Sundays, she hasn't been going.

"First thing tomorrow morning after your meds. Now go to sleep."

I turn off the lamp near her bed and pretend to catch the kiss she blows me across the room. Shutting her door, I blow out a breath, slip my high heels off, and head for the kitchen where I leave my shoes. I almost whimper with relief when I slide my feet into the black Converse sneakers that are at least five years old.

The kitchen in our small ranch house on the edge of town is a disaster. Helena works at a coffeehouse an hour away and must have been up early to work her freelance video editing gig. I may pay her tuition for school to keep her going, but she works two jobs to pay for her books, car payment for the car she uses to get to school, her car insurance, and her own medical insurance on the government exchange. Mom gets Medicaid because of disability, thank the stars, but Helena and I have to scrape enough for our health insurance since our forms for help are still processing. It's a lot to pay for when you're nineteen, but she never complains. Working two jobs while taking classes isn't easy, so I don't bust her chops too much when she leaves cereal bowls with slightly curdled milk in the sink and open cereal boxes or bags of chips on the counter.

I put the cereal away, quickly wipe down the counter with a bleach wipe, and walk to the laundry room to get a load of threadbare towels out of the dryer. It's Christmas Eve, and I'm still folding towels. The laundry is never-ending. Now I know how Mom felt when we were kids and Dad still lived at home. There's always something to wipe down in the kitchen and always laundry to do.

Grabbing the laundry basket and walking back to the kitchen, I open the fridge and grab an almost empty carton of generic egg nog from the top shelf, pour the last of a bottle of cheap vodka into the open spout, and swish the carton as I walk to the living room with the nog in one hand and the laundry basket under the other arm.

I may as well watch something on the neighbor's Wi-Fi. They can finally afford Internet, and we suck off the teat of their Wi-fi password. They don't mind because Mom brought them vegetables from the garden for decades when they were broke. They shopped at the food pantry for years when they were between jobs, and food pantries don't have a lot of fresh vegetables for the kids. Mom kept them in carrots, green beans, tomatoes, and cucumbers for years, even canning tomatoes for winter soups. Mom would also find deals on apples every fall and can jars upon jars of applesauce, always sharing it with the neighbors. When Mom got sick, the gardening and canning stopped. But the neighbors eventually found work and repaid the kindness with Internet access.

Christmas Eve in style.

I plop on the beige couch, looking through the cushions and my mother's million red throw pillows for the remote. Always red pillows at Christmas. Pink for Easter. Green around St. Patrick's Day. Orange for Halloween. You can tell the time of year in the Hepperdine house by the thrift store pillows on the couch.

"Alright, Sam and Dean. What are we hunting this time?" I ask the void as I flip to *Supernatural*. I've seen the show enough to know exactly what happens, but it's my comfort show. It's the show I watch when I'm alone on Christmas Eve and drinking the last of spiked eggnog while folding decade-old towels. I should probably watch a Christmas show of some kind, but I can't bring myself to see all the happy couples in Hallmark movies. Not when I'm so alone.

Those small-town lives are nothing like the one I lead. No grouchy lumberjack in a flannel shirt is going to save Holly Hepperdine. I'd be open to it, but there aren't any Christmas tree farmers, diner owners, or numb big-city executives in the vicinity, ready to sweep me off my feet.

I glance to the corner where our Christmas tree stands, proudly decorated, and smile briefly at it. With Mom sick and Helena so busy, I put up the tree and decorated it the best I could. Ornaments Helena and I made in Brownies or grade school hang from the branches, an eclectic jumble of salt dough and glitter. Silver tinsel hangs from the branches, and I mentally note a few spots where I could fluff it to stand out. White Christmas lights wrap around the branches, illuminating the room well enough that I turn off the nearby lamp and inhale, relaxing in the ambiance that only comes in a dark room with Christmas lights.

I settle back onto the pillows, pull a throw blanket on top of me, and take the last swig from the egg nog carton, even swishing it around in my mouth to savor the last bit of it. My mind wanders as I swallow the nog, wondering how spiked vodka nog would have compared to the taste of Jasper's cock.

Fuck, he was hot. He's all I've been able to think about since he gave me that candy cane and walked out of my jerk-off room with a wave and a big smile. I never drool on a dick. I just lube it up and give it the required yank.

But him…I wanted to *please* him. I wanted to make his session the dirtiest and smarmiest hand job he's ever received. I even surprised myself when I spit on him. I've done a lot of dirty activities in my adult life, but watching my spit dribble down that man's gorgeous dick was surreal.

And his dick was gorgeous. Beautiful with a great curve that would destroy a woman when it rubs her G-spot. It wasn't ugly at all like some dicks are. Even his pubic hair was trimmed and tasteful. His length was a good seven inches of thick glory, weeping with pre-cum on the head. If I thought I wouldn't get fired, I would have taken the whole thing in my mouth and sucked the stress he mentioned straight out of him.

But Linda One has repeatedly warned us about throat gonorrhea, and that shit sounds scary as hell.

That smile. Fuck me, that smile crushed my heart, and the sounds he made as I stroked him will fill my bean flick bank for months.

Where did he come from? Maybe I should have asked when he asked my name. If we were getting personal, I could have asked if he's staying at his grandmother's house in town for the holiday. I've never seen him before, but now I'm scared I won't ever see him again.

I pull the blanket around me tighter, shivering a little. No use getting upset about a guy I didn't know this morning, for fuck's sake. My eyes are heavy, and my arms and hands are tired from my workday. I think about rubbing one out to thoughts of Jasper, but my eyes droop.

I must fall asleep because I wake up to the credits rolling. Sitting up, I look around the room. Everything seems fine. The next episode automatically loads on the TV, and everything's as I left it.

Something woke me, and something in the back of my mind is off. A sound? A knock at the door? I pick up the baby monitor I have for Mom and shake it. No static. No noise from Mom's room. Hitting it lightly with my palm, it sputters static, but is otherwise silent.

Getting off the couch, I walk to the window, tiptoeing in case it's an intruder. The driveway is empty except for my old, black Chevy truck I bought second-hand when I graduated college and needed some kind of vehicle. Helena's car isn't there, so it wasn't her making the noise. She's probably out with friends like a normal nineteen-year-old.

A scratching sound comes from the ceiling, startling me. "Fucking squirrels," I yell, huffing off to the laundry room for the broom. It took forever for the pest guy to get rid of the squirrels the last time they got in the attic. Just what I need. "Fuck off!" I bang the ceiling with the broom handle, and I must have scared them off. Maybe I gave the squirrel a heart attack or caused it to run out of whatever entrance it has into my attic.

Throwing the broom down, I stomp back to the couch. "That'll be another six hundred bucks. Fuck my life. I'll have to give a senator hand jobs and take the hush money to pay for that work."

The scratching on the ceiling starts again, and I shake my head. The sound moves across the room and around the chimney. I squint at the top of the fireplace mantle and think. If that's a squirrel, it's a big mother fucker. If it's near the chimney, there's probably a hole in the chimney where it's coming in. Great. That's a chimney sweep visit.

The animal stops at the chimney, but there's another sound that sounds like a person grumbling to themselves. A moment later, a distinctive grunt comes from the chimney.

That was not a fucking squirrel.

There's someone on my roof. This is worse than squatting rodents.

Terror floods my veins, and I freeze. My knees tremble. My bladder suddenly feels full, and I squeeze my knees together in terror, trying not to fall on the floor and trying not to piss myself. My heart pounds out of my chest. There's a murderer on my roof, and he's going to come down the chimney. At least the murderer has a sense of humor if he's coming into the house like Santa Claus on Christmas Eve. He can be known as the Santa serial killer.

It's a good schtick for a killer, I guess.

Pebbles drop to the ground as pieces of brick and old bird nests fall through the grate. More grunting. A curse word. I tilt my head, straining my ears. The voice is...sexy. Great. I'm going to be murdered by a hot serial killer with a morbid sense of humor.

Legs appear in front of me, and I look for a weapon, not finding one. Why don't I have a weapon? I make a mental note to buy a big fucking gun if I survive this. Wait. I don't know how to use a gun. OK, I'm going to buy a big fucking machete if I survive this.

Tight red pants over chiseled thighs appear. Is this guy really dressed like Santa? This just keeps getting worse.

With a grunt, the guy pulls himself through the fireplace and appears, bent over and on all fours. He smacks dust from his suit, and I lament the filthy state of my chimney. If I wasn't so terrified, I'd be embarrassed. I work hard to make sure there's little dust and dirt in the house.

When he stands up, soot streaks his forehead and cheeks, but I still recognize him. My heart pounds so hard that I worry it'll pound straight out of my chest. It doesn't pound in fear. It pounds in shock and excitement. Maybe even a little horniness.

"Jasper?"

"Hi, Holly." He gives a small wave. "I'm glad you're up. I need a little help. And, well, I bet you're wondering why I didn't just knock. Would you believe me if I told you that I thought it would be weird?"

Anger replaces my excitement. I grit my teeth and ball my hands into fists. Is he stalking me? Is he mental? He must be if he's sliding down chimneys of girls who jerk him off for money. What kind of maniac does that? "What the fuck are you doing here?" I ask. "Did you follow me?"

"I did not follow you. I just happen to...know where you live." He bites his lip and puts his hands on his hips as he looks around my living room. "Somehow, when I say it, that sounds worse."

I back away from him until my ass hits the wall with a thump, and my legs tremble so hard that I'm worried I'll slide down the drywall. My neck hits the thermostat, and I quickly check to make sure I don't accidentally turn up the heat. My eyes flick to my cell phone on the table near the couch where I left it when I came home. Can I get to it in time to call Sheriff DeWitt? I curse when I realize it's dead anyway. I was going to charge it before bed.

Jasper moves between me and the table. Should I yell for Mom and have her use the old flip phone she keeps for emergencies? How would I even explain? Would he hurt her? Her sound machine blocks out most noise. I doubt she'd even hear my scream.

"Why the fuck did you come down the chimney?" I yell. "Most stalkers use the fucking door or a window. If you were normal, you'd jump me in the parking lot on my way to work! Are you trying to be cute? Do you think this is funny?"

He puts his hands out in front of him like he's trying to calm a wild bear. Is he as afraid of me as I am of him? That seems weird. He's the stalker. "Whoa. I can explain, Holly."

I pick up a nearby Time magazine I borrowed from the library and roll it up. Logically, I know hitting his nose with a magazine like he's a dog that pissed on the carpet isn't much of a defense plan, but it'll have to do. I hold it in front of me like a sword. "Start talking, asshole. How do you know where I live?"

He bites his lip and keeps his hands out in front of him. "I've always known where you live. I was born with the ability to find anyone."

"What the absolute fuck are you talking about?"

"I'm Santa!" he yells, matching my voice pitch and volume.

Silence fills the room, and my vision tunnels. I drop the rolled-up magazine, and it flops to the floor like a dead fish. My hands scrabble against the wall, looking for something to hold on to, but I have no idea why. Is this a dream?

He blows out a sigh and pinches the bridge of his nose. "Technically, I'm not Santa yet. Not until my father dies. The first-born son is always born with a mental list of who's naughty and who's nice. We can find anyone to deliver gifts. That's why Santa can find children on vacation to deliver their toys."

My mouth won't move. I feel it hanging open, and I'd catch flies if it was this open at a picnic in July. My eyes are dry from not blinking, and they feel like they're popping out of my skull.

"You're Santa's son?" I ask in a whisper. "Santa's real?"

"Glad you could join the conversation. Yes to both."

"The Easter Bunny?"

He shakes his head. "Not real. Just the candy companies wanting a Santa-like gimmick in the spring to increase quarterly earnings during a slow period of the year."

"The tooth fairy?"

"Just your parents trying to sweeten the pot for kids to get it over with and pull the loose tooth."

"Why are you here if you're Santa's son? Shouldn't your father be sliding down the chimney? I don't understand," I say. "This is wild. It's insane! I'm not even a child. I haven't received gifts from Santa in years."

"We still track adults on the naughty and nice list. Technically, I can track a person after childhood, even if they don't get a gift. I mean, you don't just drop out of my head once you hit eighteen. Some adults still get gifts if they specifically write to us. We're in the business of bringing happiness to anyone that asks."

"Am I on the naughty list?"

"Not really. Sure, you do some naughty things. I mean, your job is naughty, but it gets overwritten by the fact that you pay for Helena's tuition and you take care of your mother like a saint. To be honest, your job isn't nearly as naughty as some of the hedge fund managers. It's definitely nicer than politicians."

"I feel violated. This is worse than a data breach. Can you read my mind? What am I thinking right now?" I ask, focusing on the first thing that pops into my head. Hotdogs. Why I think about hotdogs, I have no idea.

"I can't read your mind. We only see actions after they happen."

I breathe out a sigh of relief that he couldn't read my thoughts from this afternoon. It'd be embarrassing for him to hear my internal monologue on his gorgeous thighs. Not to mention I've thought a lot about his dick since he left the parlor. "Good because I have no idea why I was thinking about hotdogs."

"I can explain everything if you sit down with me," he says, gesturing to the couch.

I shuffle to the couch and sit, hands stiffly at my side. "Talk. Explain."

He sits next to me and puts his arm around me like we're on a date at the movies. He turns his body a little toward me and tries to meet my eyes. I stare straight ahead, though. I'm not sure if I'm ready to accept everything here.

"I'm Santa's son."

"Got that."

"My dad is sick and has been for a few years. It was a mild illness at first. He was still able to do most of everything required to be Santa. He maintained the list, worried over the stock, and instructed the elves."

I put my face in my hands. "Fuck! The elves are real too?"

"Yep. But they're not little. I don't know where that idea came from. It's kind of offensive. Most of them are even taller than me."

"Do they wear green tights and shit?"

"Is it weird if I say yes?"

"I think all of this is weird."

"Fair point," he mumbles, looking forward. "I'll get the elves new uniforms."

"Probably a good idea. Here's an idea – go business casual."

"They'd probably like that." He rubs his nose, and his eyes settle on my Christmas tree. "As I was saying, Dad is really sick. He couldn't make the toy delivery run this year, and the stress of having to do it for the first time is why I went to get a massage today. Basically, I can't find my ass with both hands in that sleigh, and I need help."

"Help? With what?" I ask.

"I think I just about have the navigation system figured out, but I can't find anything in the sleigh. The inventory is fucked. I can't navigate *and* screw with the inventory, and I'm not sure how Dad has done this by himself for, well, since my grandfather died."

"I have questions," I say.

"I'll answer them all."

"Do you really live at the North Pole?"

"That's your first question?"

"I'm an accountant by trade. I'm all about the logistics. I need to hear logistics so I can wrap my head around the rest of this bullshit. Do you live at the magnetic North Pole?"

"No."

We stare at each other for a few moments. "OK...where are you from?"

"Canada."

"Santa lives in Canada?"

"Surprise!" Jasper sings wiggling his fingers. "We don't live near Toronto or anything, but humans can't exactly live at the North Pole, you know? We're in rural Canada and just south of the Hudson Bay in Ontario."

"Silly me. Why would I think there was anything magical about any of this?"

"Would you want to live at the North Pole?" he asks.

"Absolutely fucking not."

"Next question," Jasper says, slapping his thighs.

"Why me? Why are you at my house?"

He sighs and looks forward, blowing out a breath I didn't know he was holding. "When I saw you today in the waiting room, something happened to me. I was like, 'That's her.' I know it's weird. I just saw you and wanted to know more about you. When you told me your name, I put it together who you were. There aren't any other women named Holly in the county around your age. I know what happened today was a business transaction with you, but it wasn't for me. I liked talking to you. I liked making you laugh. I knew I wanted to see you again outside of your work."

"If we're being honest, you were the shiny spot of my day. But Santa's son? Ontario? You know who I am and where I live. I need a minute to get my head around this." I wave my hands in a circle "I mean, you can't just drop down my chimney and tell me you have the magic power to see when I blew my history professor in college and then ask me on a date."

He looks at his watch and cringes. "Uh, that's the thing, Holly."

"What now?"

"I want to see you again. I mean, it's all I've thought about since I left this afternoon. But I was kind of hoping you could get your head around this faster because I need your help."

I scoot away from him and stare. "What kind of help?"

"I was kind of hoping you could run inventory for me while I navigate tonight."

Laughter bubbles up from my chest, and I look around the room. "Am I on a hidden camera show? Did they reboot *Punk'd* and start with punking a tugger from rural Pennsylvania?"

Jasper furrows his brow with a confused look. Maybe he didn't watch much TV as a kid. Damn those sexy eyes, though. "So, you won't consider helping me tonight?"

"Why me? I realize we have a connection, but if you know so much about me, why don't you just call me for coffee next week? Spoiler alert. If you'd done that, I would have gone."

He smiles, straightening his shoulders like he's ecstatic I said I would go on a date with him. He shakes his head, probably thinking about my question. "Holly, I picked you because I haven't met anyone that has made me feel butterflies in a long time. That, and I can see your education. You're an accountant by trade. I need *your* help, and I didn't know where else to turn."

Chapter 4

JASPER

"This is fucking nuts!" Holly yells a foot from Blitzen's face.

I quickly clamp my hand over her mouth and look around at the other houses in her neighborhood. No lights are on, and I jerk my head toward her neighbor's house across the street. Thankfully, she gets the idea that she has to be quiet, and she zips her lips when I move my hand away, miming throwing away a key.

"You have to be quiet. This is Blitzen," I whisper, stroking my hand down the side of Blitzen's head. Her red collar jingles, and she blows steam out of her snout.

"They're all real?"

"Most of the stories are a little off. For example, there's no Rudolph." I jerk my chin toward the front of the sleigh where there isn't a lone reindeer with a light-up nose. "That was just one silly story. The rest of the reindeer are real enough, though. They're actually caribou, but I realize the rest of the world calls them reindeer because of the stories."

"How long do reindeer live?"

"If you're wondering if it's the same Blitzen that was named ages ago, the answer is no. They're like my family. The oldest female born to a sleigh reindeer gets the title of Blitzen or Dasher or Dancer after their mothers die."

"Females?"

"Here's your science lesson for the day. Male reindeer drop their antlers in the late fall around November. Females drop their antlers in the spring. If a reindeer still has antlers in December, it's probably female." I nod around to the crew of reindeer, patiently waiting for direction on Holly's roof. Prancer shakes her head a bit. She's always hated the bridle.

"I learned something new today," she says, shivering in the night air. I'd go back in for her coat, but once I get her in the sleigh, she'll be fine with the butt warmers built into the seats, the stack of blankets, and the hot cocoa bar my mother installed in the console.

"You learned something besides the fact that my family is real?"

She smiles and relaxes her shoulders for the first time since I slid down the chimney. She's taking this better than I thought she would. "Fine, I guess I've learned two things."

"Let me show you the sleigh!"

I grab Holly's hand and pull her to my pride and joy. Well, it's the pride and joy of the family. Now I know what normal guys feel like when they buy a Lamborghini and go pick up their girl. Pride blossoms in my chest, and I pull my shoulders back and smile as I pat the side of the sleigh. "Here it is, the family jewel."

Holly doesn't notice my pride or demeanor. She's too busy staring at the sleigh, blinking and moving her mouth like a fish. She wants to say something but isn't sure she can form the words. She reaches out a shaky hand and runs it across the top of the candy-apple-red wood.

She stops and fingers the leather reins that are tied off through a loop I use when we make stops.

She pulls her finger back like something burned her. "It's like what Charles used to control the horse on *Little House on the Prairie*."

"Get in," I say. "It's cold out here, and Mom always makes cocoa. I also have some of those heated handwarmer things you can stick in your pockets."

She steps into the sleigh with wide eyes. "This comes with everything, huh?"

"All the bells and whistles. Do you want to drive it? I'll help you hold the reins."

She shakes her head like she's scared and sticks her hands under her butt. Her eyes are wide, and she looks at the houses around us. "Can they see us?"

"Kind of. People can see it, but it doesn't register in their minds. If someone looked out their window right now, they wouldn't be like, 'Hey, Mildred, there's a sleigh on top of the Hepperdine house.' They'd see it, blink, and go right back to what they were doing, not letting it faze them."

"How am I seeing it then?"

"I'm allowing it. Yeah, I can do that too. At least while I'm wearing the suit."

I take the reins and make a whistling noise that all the reindeer, except for Prancer, obey. That's why Prancer gets put at the back of the sleigh. She's obstinate, and the rest of the reindeer pull her along. The sleigh lilts to the side like it usually does when eight reindeer lift into the air and find their rhythm. Holly grabs onto my arm, and I chuckle as I pat her hand with my free one. "It's fine. You won't fall out."

She looks over the side. "I guess now would be a bad time to tell you that I'm afraid of heights."

"What happens when you get onto a high building?"

"I puke. I even get sick on airplanes if I'm near the window. I don't suppose you have barf bags in this thing?"

"Just look straight ahead. It'll be a nice view. Promise."

We rise off her roof several feet and then zip right at about forty miles per hour. It's not the fastest speed we can go, but Holly still screams and grips my arm and the bar in front of her, holding on for dear life. "Has any Santa ever died on Christmas?"

"Not by falling off the sleigh. There was the Santa that got shot during the Civil War. That was in 1863, and they came up with the suit idea then. Other than that, a dog mauled my great-grandfather." I shudder at the thought. I was raised to be afraid of big dogs because of the family trauma surrounding that incident.

She takes deep breaths through her nose, and tears form in her eyes. "You have to give me a minute. I learned Santa's real and that I spit on his son's dick today, female reindeer pull the sleigh, and I'm currently a hundred feet above my neighborhood. Talk to me about something mundane. No magic allowed."

I nod and turn the sleigh to the right again, setting off in the direction to start delivering my packages. At least, I think I'm going the right way. I want to take a few minutes to get Holly used to the sleigh. If we fly around for a few minutes, maybe she'll relax.

"You're probably wondering why I chose rural Pennsylvania," I say, trying to keep it mundane like she asked.

"Good. Let's start with that."

"I'm an Eagles fan. Huge. I was here for the last game since Dad got me season tickets last year, and I just went for a ride outside of Philadelphia. I'm not used to big cities, even though I love my football team. So, I got in my rental car and just kind of drove around, sipping coffee and thinking. I ate at a truck stop and drove further down the interstate until I saw a rickety old sign with your parlor mentioned. I guess I thought getting a massage would help me with the stress. I certainly didn't expect…" I trail off and look at her. Damn, I want to kiss her cheeks. They're so pink in the cold. "Well, I didn't expect you and didn't expect what happened."

She tentatively looks over the side of the sleigh and quickly moves back to sitting up straight. She looks ahead and takes a deep breath through her nose as she closes her eyes. "Do you know everything about me?"

I don't want to scare her. "I know enough."

"What does that mean?"

"Let's just say, I could probably dive into your past enough to avoid some of the awkward first date questions you may not want to answer."

She looks at me, curious. I'm just glad she's not barfing or hyperventilating. If I can keep her talking, maybe she will relax and help me. "Elaborate," she says.

"I know your dad did a runner a few years back. You pay for Helena's school. By the way, she's on the nice list. Your whole family is, so I know you have a nice family." I turn the reins left and open the console compartment with packages of cocoa and a hot pot full of water. I hit the hot pot button to get the water boiling. "I know you have an accounting degree that you don't use, and I can kind of piece together why. It's the little things I don't know."

"Little things?"

"Your favorite food. Your preferences about certain things. Basically, anything that happens in your head. I can't see that. I can only see things you do. Actions."

"So, you really have no idea what I'm thinking right now?" she asks, squinting hard like she's sending me a telepathic message.

"Nope. Is it hotdogs again?"

She blushes and licks her lips but turns to face the console, suddenly interested in the cocoa packets and mini marshmallows. She picks up a mug and taps it, waiting for the water to be done heating. "Not hotdogs, but it's in the universe of wieners."

"What's your favorite color?" I ask, changing the subject to something mundane. I'll get a stiffy if I think about her thinking about wieners.

"Blue. Let me guess yours. Red?"

"Nope," I say, shaking my head. "Eagles green. What's your favorite food?"

"My mother's spaghetti. She adds a smidge of hot sauce to the sauce. Nobody comes close to getting it like hers. Yours? If you tell me candy canes, I'm going to have you turn this sleigh around simply because of your twee bullshit."

"Toast."

She sputters a laugh. "You're Santa's son, and your favorite food is toast?"

"I never claimed to make sense. There's nothing like crispy toast with butter on top. Peanut butter on toast is also nice, but I have to be in the mood."

She smiles again, and I could stare at it for a week. It's like the time I was delivering toys with Dad in Italy and we stopped in Florence to see *David*. It was such a beautiful piece of art. I have the same thoughts about Holly – a beautiful piece of art. Precious and priceless.

"So, it's the suit that's magic? How does that work?"

"Yeah, I guess I mentioned that but didn't really explain, huh? Yes. It's the suit that does most of the Christmas sparkle. The sleigh is magic, but I can't take the sleigh power with me into the house. At the end of the day, I'm only human. I can get in and out of houses with the suit. It also helps me manipulate time."

"You can manipulate time?"

"Only in the suit. I can move super-fast if I want and slow things down around me at the same time. How do you think I deliver so many toys in one night?"

"That was the one thing that made me rethink Santa when I was young. I couldn't work that out or imagine it."

"It's usually the finisher when kids sit down and think about it. However, you'd be surprised at how few kids both write to us and are on the nice list. It's a requirement that they write to us if they want a gift. Again, I can't see wants or preferences. I'm not a mind reader. The kids that aren't on the nice list or don't write to us still get presents from their parents. Most kids don't even notice they're not on Santa's list. The vast majority of children don't believe by the time they're ten anyway. They stop writing. Some cultures don't recognize Santa at all. It's not millions of children."

"So, you don't have to deliver billions of toys tonight?"

"I'm delivering 156,341 gifts this year. I just get in the house, drop the gifts, leave a bite mark on a cookie, take a swig of milk, and get the fuck out. I may take a carrot for a reindeer if the family leaves them out. I give them to the *good reindeer*." I enunciate the last words and glare at Prancer.

This is insane. I'm spilling all the family secrets to this woman. I've never told anyone this. Granted, I've never really had to tell anyone before. All my friends were elves growing up, so no explanation was necessary. I never dated someone around Christmas or even dated seriously enough to tell them what I did for a living. Most women I've known think I'm a freelance graphic designer.

I have no idea why that was the first thing that popped into my head when I had to think of a profession on the spot, but it's believable, unlike being Santa's heir.

The hot pot squeals, and Holly reaches for it. She pours a cup of hot water for herself, sets her cup on the shelf, and pours one for me. "Marshmallows?" she asks.

"Always."

She pours the cocoa packet into the water and spoons several mini marshmallows on the top. Handing it to me, she flashes a smile. I take it from her and blow on the mug.

"Feel better?" I ask.

"A little. Maybe this would be a good time to explain what you need my help with."

I jerk my thumb to the backseat. "Are you sure you're ready for me to explain that hot mess?"

"I guess it's as good a time as any."

Chapter 5

HOLLY

I can't remember the last time I wanted to throw up like this but didn't actually do it. It's the same feeling as being so drunk that the room spins. You know you'll feel better if you throw up. You may even go to the toilet and hover over it, hoping that you can just get it over with. Nothing comes out of me. It's just a miserable feeling at the top of my stomach.

I look over the edge again as the sleigh rocks a little, spilling the hot cocoa. Should I hold on to Jasper? Is that too forward? Then again, I've already seen his dick. Clutching his arm wouldn't be so intimate.

Gently, I loop my arm through his. I don't pull or use a firm touch. I don't want to throw off his driving or startle him while he's driving the reindeer. But it's nice when he smiles and looks at me for a split second.

Why do I feel like he's the only guy that's really seen me? He can see my actions – and I'm still not sure how he does that – but I feel like he *sees* me. He looks at me like we're old friends and like I'm the only woman in the world.

"There's a navigation system I use, and it's working fine," he says, blowing on his mug of cocoa.

I take the cocoa from him so he has his hands free, and I blow on it for him. His face reddens when I hand it back to him. Maybe he thought of me blowing on something else.

"What do you need me for?"

"I can't do it all myself and get it done tonight, even with my ability to manipulate time. I can navigate and drive, but the stock is fucked up beyond anything I've ever seen. The elves have organized it to my dad's preferences, but it doesn't make any sense to me. It's not by geographic region and alphabetical. I have stuff that goes to Canada next to Romania. It's nuts. I went on a few runs with my dad as a kid, but he never really explained the stock. I need someone to organize and find things for me. Back there." He jerks his head to the back of the sleigh.

I slowly turn and squint. "Are you telling me that every toy is back in that little sleigh? You don't deliver and then go back for more?"

"No time for that."

"Oh, Lord." I put my cocoa down and turn in my seat. Maybe I can focus on stock so it takes my mind off falling out of a flying sleigh and dying a horrific death. "I'll pop back there and take a look."

"Thanks, Holly. You can use the ladder."

I shake my head and blink my eyes, startled. "Ladder? How is there a ladder?"

"Oh, the sleigh is magic, so it looks small. Once you get in there, there's actually a large warehouse in it."

"Why?"

He shrugs. "That's the way it's always been. It makes sense when you think about it. I mean, it would be weird to drive a huge flying warehouse."

I look around the sleigh pulled by reindeer, a gorgeous man in a Santa suit, the cocoa in the dashboard, and the storage area in the back that has a ladder in it. "We wouldn't want to be weird or ridiculous, would we?"

"Nope." Jasper smiles, and I want to reach out and palm his face. Slide my finger down his nose. Hell, I just want to touch him in some way.

I pat him on the arm and turn to the stock area of the sleigh. Presents sit at the top, and they look like they've been wrapped by a professional gift-wrapping legion of elves with their perfect creases, seemingly invisible tape, and perfect velvet bows. "Do I just crawl in?" I ask.

"Just get in there. Once you're in, watch your step. The first one's a doozy."

I have to be dreaming. This is a hallucination brought on by bad egg nog or reading too much *Alice in Wonderland* as a child.

I throw my leg over the back of the sleigh, bring my other leg with it, and sit on the edge for a moment, taking deep breaths and trying to decide if I'm more afraid of falling since there's nothing to hold on to up here or more afraid of diving into a pile of gifts that's really a hidden warehouse.

Tentatively, I kick aside some gifts until my foot hits something. "Holy shit, there is a ladder."

"Told you," Jasper says, turning the sleigh to the right and landing on a roof with a thump. I expect to be jostled around like being unbuckled in an airplane, but I only lean a little to the left. At least Jasper is a good driver of this thing.

"Is this a stop?"

"Yep. I thought we'd handle houses around your county first since we're here. It'll let you get used to departures and landings until you get your air legs, so to speak. I don't want to just throw you into deliveries in New York. You need to get back there and find..." His voice trails off as he checks his list. He squints at the tablet on the console that's some kind of spreadsheet with names and statuses on it. I glance over Jasper's shoulder for a closer look and see a lot of kids marked as naughty. "Find Madison Luther."

I look at the houses around me. We're in a blue-collar neighborhood much like my own, and a few lights are on down the street. The house across from us has the porch light on. Anyone could look out and see us. "I may be a long time, Jasper. I'm not used to this. What if they see?"

"Remember the magic suit and the magic sleigh." He pats his chest, and I shiver. I'm not sure if I shiver from the cold, fear of going into the sleigh, or because he looks so damn hot in his magic suit.

"Be right back. I'll see if I can find Martin Luther."

"Naughty list in 1517. You need *Madison* Luther."

I make a finger gun at him. "Right. Madison. Incidentally, was Martin Luther on the naughty list for going against the Catholic Church? Just curious. This is historically fascinating."

"Vandalism. He shouldn't have nailed his issues to someone else's door."

"Huh. I guess it's too bad they didn't have tape back then."

He smiles, and I smile back before taking a deep breath, closing my eyes, and inching into the sleigh stock area.

As soon as I'm past the decoy presents on top, the room turns into something that looks like Home Depot. Rows of large shelves have pallets on them, but instead of boxes of products, the pallets contain huge cardboard containers that are filled with presents. Small golf carts with trailers on the back of them, probably for moving presents, are scattered throughout the room.

I climb down the ladder and realize it's not my last time climbing tonight. Ladders run across the shelves like in old libraries, and I guess that's how I'll get to the presents on high shelves.

"OK, Holly, you can do this. Madison Luther. Madison Luther in rural Pennsylvania. How the hell do I find this kid?"

I walk to the end of the first row and cross my fingers that this place is like Home Depot with signs with what's in an aisle clearly displayed on the endcap. Thankfully, this is the case.

Lebanon.

Well, that won't do right now. We're in Pennsylvania, nowhere near Lebanon. Are the shelves countries that are arranged in alphabetical order? I walk to the next aisle.

Iceland.

I see what Jasper meant. The shelves aren't alphabetical, and they aren't even sorted by continent. Hell, they're not even sorted by climate.

I tap my foot and think. How would this make sense? Closing my eyes, I think about an older man. An older Santa. Was he used to doing things the way *his* father taught him? Did Jasper's grandfather do things the way *he* was taught? I should have asked Jasper for more information. How does this shelving make sense?

I walk to the next shelf.

Vietnam/Laos/Cambodia.

I blow out a frustrated growl and move to the next aisle as something itches at my brain. All of this sounds like something I may have learned in high school or in my college general education classes I had to take before I started accounting. Is this by something historical?

Something that would have meant something to a Santa and the Santas that came before them?

Korea/North and South.

My brain snaps to life, and a hypothesis forms. I turn in the other direction, snapping my fingers as I walk to break the silence of the warehouse. My shoes squeak against the floor as I walk, and my snapping fingers echo off every wall. If I'm right...

If I'm right, the United States will be further toward the back. If Saint Nicholas lived during the Roman Empire, the system may have started with the Empire and evolved as countries came into existence. Sure, St. Nicholas wasn't known as a jolly man who delivered gifts using reindeer back then, but it's all I have to work with. I'll bet Helena's next tuition check that England, France, and Portugal are toward the back with the United States somewhere in between, gaining its independence in the late 1700s.

"Please be right," I say, walking faster down the shelves. "I don't have any other ideas."

The countries of Latin America appear. I have to be on the right track. This is right. I can feel it. They had things sorted by countries and territories centuries ago, and they just added shelves as countries came about.

The United States appears in front of me. If the same theory applies, it won't be alphabetical by state. It'll be by when the state became a state. I certainly don't know those dates by heart, but that theory holds water when I find Hawaii and Alaska toward the front. Pennsylvania is nestled in the back with the other original colonies.

Looking around, I spot a golf cart next to a hook with coats, scarves, and bib overalls, and I smile when I notice the keys are still in the cart.

"Well, you're in luck," I say, popping my head out of the decoy presents and scaring Jasper. He jumps and sloshes cocoa on his suit. In front of us, Prancer bucks and kicks her feet, narrowly missing the front of the sleigh.

"Did you find Pennsylvania and Madison Luther?"

I hold up Madison Luther's present over my head like it's a bowling trophy. "Found it. And I have most of the presents in our area in the cart right below this ladder. I also figured out your dad's system."

"What is it?"

"Independence and statehoods. Let's not fuss over it. I have it figured out. I may need to Google some stuff to find things tonight, but I know what I'm looking for now."

He blows out a sigh, and his shoulders relax. "I'm so glad I met you. You're a genius, Holly. Sheer genius. I would never have guessed that."

"Yeah, just think how awful it would have been if you'd received a hand job from a woman who didn't pay attention in history class. We need to get going, though. Go do your thing."

He puts his cup down. "Are you ready?"

"Ready for what? Staying with the reindeer and having you bring me any leftover cookies? Yes."

"Nice try," he says as he wraps the reins around the handle and jumps from the sleigh. "You're coming with me."

Chapter 6

JASPER

"The fuck I am," she says.

"Look, Dad has done this for years. He's in and out. I'm still new at this and worried about getting caught."

"You have the suit. Won't people just look at you and not even remember they see you?"

"Dogs can see me. They can give it away."

She puts her hands on her hips and blows out a sigh that moves her bangs. "Is there anything else you need to tell me about how all this works?" she asks.

"I think that's it."

"I know everything there is to know here?"

"Yes."

"You want me to act as some kind of dog lookout now?"

I nod. "Uh-huh."

"This is the last thing you get to ask for here, Jasper. You can't just throw all of this at someone, ask them to figure out an archaic stocking system, and then ask them to work as a dog lookout. Clear?"

"Understood. I completely agree. In fact, I think you get an ask sometime tonight."

"Like a favor to call in?" She blushes, and my dick throbs in my pants.

Oh, please let her ask for a favor where my dick gets to do stuff. Please. If we weren't under such a time crunch, I'd bend her over and eat her from the back right on this roof. My hands flex like I want to hold her hand or touch her in some way. I'm like a kid in middle school that can't keep from getting an erection from a pat on the shoulder from the cute girl I like.

And why wouldn't I like her? She must be brilliant to figure out my dad's stock system. She's brave enough to get on the sleigh. She draws boundaries when she has to put her foot down. I tilt my head to the side, smiling. "Do you know what favor you want to call in, Holly?"

She clears her throat. "I'm forming an idea. We'll see how the night progresses."

The air crackles between us, and I shove my hands into my pockets before I touch her inappropriately. The tension, the way her eyes darken, and her blush give her away. My dick is totally going to get to do stuff.

I nod. "Right. Let's get to work."

"Do I just slide down after you?" she asks, nodding toward the chimney. "What if I fall?"

"You won't fall. I go first, and I'll catch you. Besides, the suit slows me down so I don't get hurt, and I can slow your fall."

She doesn't answer me. She doesn't tell me it's fine or flat-out refuse. She gets out of the sleigh and walks over to the chimney, knocking on the brick like it's a door or like she's checking if it's sturdy. I grab Madison Luther's present and stomp through the snow to the chimney, straighten my suit, and move down the chimney like I've been taught.

I come out at the bottom into a dark room. Weird. Most people usually leave the Christmas lights on or something. A lamp. Low kitchen track lighting. A nightlight. It's pitch black in here, and I turn and wave Holly down the chimney. She cringes before swinging her legs over the chimney. She slides fast and doesn't shriek on her way down. Another point for her. Pride builds in my chest for her. This woman is amazing.

"Where do you want me to stand?" she asks, blinking as her eyes adjust to the darkness.

"Over by the living room entrance. They have a dog. Tell me if you see it."

She grips my arm. Normally, I'd love that, but something about her grip is panicked. Her nails rake my skin and not in the way I'd want them scraping up my back during a good fuck. Something's wrong.

"I think it's too late, Jasper."

My eyes adjust, and there's a sliver of moonlight coming through the curtains. It's just enough light to see the large Doberman standing in the entryway. Even if we didn't see him, the low growl is enough for me to know that we've already been spotted.

Panicking, I throw Madison's gift to the Christmas tree in the corner, not even caring if the item inside is fragile. It lands with a clunking sound, but I don't give it a second thought. Fear moves up my spine. I grew up with reindeer, moose, and fox. I like most dogs, even after my great-grandfather's unfortunate mauling, but when they growl at me when I'm intruding in their home, they scare me.

"Don't be scared," Holly whispers, releasing her grip on me and taking deep breaths. "They can smell fear."

"I have fear. I stink with it," I say as the growl gets louder. "I stink. I stink."

"Shhh," she hisses just as lights flick on, blinding us.

The dog lets out a low bark, stares at us, and points like a hunting dog. A bare-chested man in his underwear blinks around the room and I grab Holly, pulling her to my chest. If my arms are around her, the man will see us but not care or mentally register it.

And I do not want to tangle with this man. He wears a gold chain around his thick neck, and he's built like a brick shithouse. I'm well-built and lift, but this man scares me. He looks like the leader of a motorcycle club or a strip club bouncer. He looks around the room while stroking his long gray beard that practically touches the gold chain over his chest.

"What is it, boy?" the man asks, looking around the room as Holly and I stand frozen and wide-eyed. "What are you barking and growling at? Another rat in here? Fuck it all, I cannot handle another rat."

The dog slinks off the couch and stalks across the room slowly, growling the entire way. I pull Holly back with me as I walk toward the chimney. The man across the room looks right at us, seeing us but not really *seeing* us.

Holly doesn't panic. She doesn't cry. Granted, her job is giving men hand jobs. She probably gets her fair share of angry customers or customers that want more. She may even know this guy. Maybe that's why she isn't scared of him. Even if she doesn't know him, fear is something she probably deals with on a daily basis. She's not a coddled boy from rural Canada who never has to worry about being attacked by a man wearing tightie whities.

The man's right hand was behind his back when he entered the room, but he swings it forward as his eyes dart side to side. He searches the room and slowly tiptoes toward us, following his dog. He holds a taser gun in his hand, and Holly pushes against my chest as we back toward the chimney. She trembles in my arms, but I'm much worse.

"T-taser!" I yell before I can stop myself.

Holly's hand flies to my mouth to shut me up, but my scream startles the dog. The man looks around confused, and the dog's odd movement toward me scares the man. Unfortunately, the taser is pointed at us when the man nearly jumps out of his skin.

Electrified prongs move toward us in what seems like slow motion, and I try to move Holly out of the way at the last second. The dog lunges forward and grabs onto my boot, which probably terrifies the man as he sees his dog clamp down on something that isn't quite there in the man's mind.

The man screams. I scream as the dog bites into my boot. Holly screams as the prongs on the taser catch her in the arm. I scream again as Holly shakes for a few seconds, her eyes rolling back and a line of drool running from her mouth.

She hits the floor with a thud because I didn't catch her in time. She's still hidden because she's slumped against me, and I do a weird dance of trying to fight off the attack dog and keep Holly out of sight. I fight with the animal and try to pry its teeth off my boot before it hits flesh. I can't imagine what's going through the man's mind as he watches his pet grab onto something and jerk it from side to side.

"What the fuck is happening?" the man screams. "What the hell did the taser even hit? Cocoa, what do you have in your mouth?"

"Holly?" I ask. I do my best to get the dog off me without hurting it, but I have to get us both out of here. Now. "Holly, are you OK?

Please be alive. Please be alive." I lightly slap her cheek. She whimpers, and I nearly piss myself with relief.

"Cocoa, stay!" the man orders as I look around for the taser prongs on Holly.

Thankfully, the man grabs the dog by the collar and drags him from the room. I pull out the taser prongs, hoping that they aren't electrically charged after the first hit. Once I get them out of Holly's body, two drops of blood drip down her arm where she was lightly punctured.

"Jasper?" she asks. "Did I piss my pants?"

I look down at her tights, the same tights she wore to work today. Christmasy. Happy. They don't look like they belong on someone that was just tased by a disgruntled homeowner. Without thinking, I lift her skirt a little to check the wetness situation like she's one of those Betsy Wetsy dolls my father told me about and put the skirt modestly back in place when I'm done. This is not how I imagined finally seeing up her skirt. "Dry as a bone."

"Well, that's good. I heard people piss or shit themselves when they get tased. I can't feel my legs. Is that normal?"

"I think so. I think you lose muscle control for a bit. Here, put your arms around me. I'll carry you out."

She does as I ask, and I pull us up. She wraps her arms around my neck, and I frown as I turn to the chimney to get us back up to the roof. If this happened at any other moment – her in my arms and looking up at me through fluttering lashes – it'd be the most romantic moment of my life.

"Don't shit on hot Santa," she mumbles, clearly not aware that she's speaking out loud. "Don't shit on Jasper."

"If you haven't already made a mess, you're probably not going to poop your pants. Let's get you back to the sleigh. I'm so sorry that happened, Holly."

"That hurt. Being Santa's dog lookout really hurts. I never want to be tased again. I'll never shoplift a lipstick or put myself in any situation where a box store security guard would do that to me."

"The funny thing is that my dad has been doing this for decades, and he's never been bit or tased. I'm a failure, Holly. Not only did I get bit, but I let you get tased."

We get back up to the roof, and I set Holly in the sleigh. She immediately slinks against the side as I get in the console and look for a water bottle. Surely, Mom would have packed water.

I finally find a bottle behind the cocoa and candy canes and uncap it. "Here, drink this. You'll feel better. Can you wiggle your toes?"

"Wiggle my toes?"

"Baby steps, right?"

She screws up her face like she's concentrating. "I think I moved my big toe. My head hurts. Is my head supposed to hurt?"

"I'm sure anything is possible," I say, pulling out my phone and Googling *taser aftercare*. "I was right to pull the prongs out after the initial electrical charge. It says you should return to normal soon but may be sore for a few days." I hop into the sleigh and show Holly my screen, which she half-ass looks at. "Do I need to take you to the hospital?"

"I don't think so. My legs are starting to tingle like they're rebooting. Just give me a few minutes. I haven't met my deductible for the year. It's too expensive if I'll be OK anyway." She leans against the side of the sleigh, whimpering again. If we were in a car, her face would be smashed up against the window. "Let's just get out of here before the man thinks that something's weird and comes up here with Cocoa to investigate."

"Not until I know you're OK." I pull a small emergency blanket packet out from under the seat. My father told me they were there in case something happens that I see or something happens directly to me. I sure didn't think I'd need it on my first delivery. I open the packet, pull the aluminum foil space-like blanket out, and drape it over here. "Here. Just in case you go into shock."

"What the hell is this?"

"Emergency blanket. It's for if you get caught in the wilderness and need warmth or if you go into shock after witnessing something traumatic. I don't want you to go into shock."

"I look like a ham sandwich."

I smile. "Holly, trust me when I tell you that you look nothing like a ham sandwich. I've never seen someone so utterly beautiful and perfect in all my life, even when you're wrapped in aluminum foil."

"You're just saying that because you feel bad I was tased."

I sigh and scoot closer to her. I tentatively reach out and wipe a tendril of her dark hair back from where it's stuck to her cheek, probably from rogue drool. "Yeah, I feel bad." I put my hand over my heart. "I feel utterly fucking destroyed that I couldn't get you out of the way in time."

She raises her head and squints. "Wait. If you were trying to push me out of the way, that would have meant you'd get tased."

"I would have taken it. One hundred percent. It's my fault you're here tonight. I needed help. But don't for a second think I find you unattractive wrapped in aluminum foil. I could have asked an ugly elf to ride with me tonight. Part of me knew you'd be able to help. You're also the most beautiful woman I've ever seen, Holly Hepperdine."

"Are you using your yearly delivery as a first date, Jasper?" She tilts her head and blinks. "What's your last name?"

"Nicholas."

She laughs a little and mumbles, "Of course. How silly of me."

"And yes, maybe I'm using this as a first date. I guess something in my brain wasn't sure how I would have stomped into the massage place and asked you out, but this seems like a better option."

"It's definitely the weirdest date I've ever been on."

"I aim for originality," I say, tilting her chin up to look at me. The snow falls lightly on her face and gets stuck in her eyelashes as she stares at me. "I wanted to be someone you remember."

She slides her hands up my chest. Even through the thick Santa suit, I tremble at her touch like I would if her hand was on my bare chest. I imagine that hand moving over my pecs, my nipples, and sliding down my abs until she reaches the cock she so expertly worked earlier today.

I can't stand it any longer. I have to taste this woman. Consume her. I lean forward, and she welcomes me with open arms. Literally. Her arms wrap around my body as I press my forehead to her and run my nose against hers, testing if she's OK with the proximity. She licks her lips, and the smallest part of her tongue hits my mouth since I'm so close to her. I whine at the feel of her and rub my lips together, trying to taste her from that small tongue flick.

She closes her eyes like she's eating really good pie, and I know she's fine with it. Her body is pliable and limp in my arms like I could do anything I want to her right now. Oh, the things I want to do to her. Sick things. Things involving every hole.

Her mouth on mine will do for now. I lean forward and press my lips to hers. As she parts her lips, we battle for dominance until she eventually gives up and lets me take control of the kiss. Our mouths mesh wildly as our hands explore. I run my thumbs up over her cheeks until her silky hair is in my fist, and her hands slide up my chest, around my neck, and fist my own hair as we pull against each other.

I come up for air and lick my lips, tasting her. "Did you have nog tonight?"

She smiles and touches my face. I lean into her palm. "Nog with a little vodka."

"I love egg nog."

She sputters a laugh, and I notice how her lips are swollen. I did that. I made her lips a wreck. Oh, how I want to wreck other parts of her. I want her hair a wild mess after I fuck her. I want her other lips swollen from being wrapped around my length. I want her to hold a bag of frozen peas against her pussy after a night with me, and I want her to smile about it and ask for more.

"You probably love all things Christmas, huh?" she asks, straightening her skirt that became bunched while we kissed. She flexes her legs, making sure they're awake after the taser. "Let me guess. You even like peppermint bark."

"And anything with coconut," I say, sitting up in my seat and grabbing the reins. Having more fun with Holly and exploring her body will have to wait. "Don't get me hard by mentioning bonbons. But that's not important. Let's get to the next house."

Chapter 7

HOLLY

"Which child do you need a toy for now?" I ask Jasper, trying to catch my breath.

Fuck, that taser hurt, but my body's still reeling from *him*. That kiss was worth a hundred tasers. If he had only slid his hand up my ridiculous skirt, he would have felt exactly how much I enjoyed him. My panties and tights are uncomfortably wet, and I wish I could ball up my soaked tights and shove them in the console, trading them for something more comfortable.

"Remember when I said we aim for happiness for anyone that asks or believes?"

"Yeah," I drawl. "Dear Lord, what now?"

"Well, this house always sends a letter. Every year. It's the Tanners. They have different tastes, and I think my father just likes that they still ask for something. It's cute. We always deliver. They're adults that know there's a Santa. They get something every year and keep asking."

"You have to be kidding me."

Jasper gestures over his shoulder toward the storage area. "Look for Darryl and Kristin Tanner."

I give him a mock salute and lean back, digging through the present pile that I pulled when I found Madison Luther's present. At the bottom of the pile, I find two presents. They're tied together, but only one of the packages, a smaller one, is for Darryl. The other package, a long, rectangular box about a foot long, is for Kristin.

I briefly shake Kristin's gift. "Is this what I think it is?"

Jasper closes his eyes like he's mentally scrolling through the inventory, and he smirks. "Yep."

"People can write to Santa for dildos?"

Jasper shrugs. "We specialize in *toys*, Holly. It's a toy. It makes them happy. Why not spread a little Christmas cheer?"

I sit back down on the seat and Jasper takes the gifts from me. His pants pockets are huge, so he shoves the toy in a pocket until I can only see the top of Kristin's present.

"Do they have a dog?" I ask.

"No dog," he says. "Should be an easy drop."

There's no chimney at the Tanner house. There's not even a flat roof to land on since the roof is steep and looks like a triangle from the side. Jasper parks the sleigh behind a crop of evergreen trees on the empty lot next to the house. I'm on high alert now. I don't need another zap, so I make sure to stay behind Jasper as he opens the front door into the living room.

"Did they leave the door unlocked?" I ask.

"No, I can get through any locked door by just touching it as long as I'm in the suit."

"This just keeps getting weirder," I whisper, tiptoeing into the house behind Jasper.

"It's a lot. But there's too much to explain all at once."

"I need one of those charts where you pick yes or no and then there's an arrow pointing to what to do next."

Jasper looks over his shoulder at me. "You've just described my entire childhood education."

The Tanners have a nice house for people that still write to Santa. The house is immaculate with folded cashmere blankets over the couch cushions. A sturdy oak coffee table is in the middle of the room, and the sectional couches are leather with cupholders and butt warmer buttons. Long stockings hang from the fireplace that's obviously fake since there's no chimney, and a large flat-screen television is mounted on the wall above me. The floorplan is open, and a quick glance at the kitchen shows granite countertops, stainless steel appliances, and a top-of-the-line expresso maker my hands itch to try.

"Are they here?" I whisper to Jasper. I want to explore more.

He shakes his head and closes his eyes, probably seeing their actions right now. "They're at a party."

I cross the living room floor and slowly sit on their leather sectional, whining with pleasure as I slink into the cushions. I've never felt anything like it. I suddenly sit up straight, afraid to put my whole weight on their couch. I don't want to leave weird butt marks on their furniture.

"Trying out the sofa?" Jasper asks. He flicks his eyes to the front door.

"Do you ever get tempted to try things out in houses?"

"This is my first run except for a few practice runs when I was a kid, but I had to stay in the sleigh."

I snap my fingers. "That's right. Does your dad ever admit to doing fun stuff in houses when the owners aren't there? Jumping on a trampoline? Making a cup of coffee in a really fancy coffee maker? Does he use their toilet if he needs to go?"

"No," he chuckles.

"I'd do it. You're all better people than most."

Jasper walks to the couch and sits next to me. "What would you do?"

"Probably what I usually do when I go to someone's house – look through the medicine cabinet."

"You do that?"

"Of course. I like seeing all the brands people use. Toothpaste. Shaving cream. Tampons. It's interesting to know their shopping habits. You don't nose around?"

"I don't need to snoop, remember? I can see actions. For example, I know the Tanners have a hidden sex room in their basement."

I sit up a little straighter. "Like a sex dungeon?"

"Yep." He closes his eyes and hums like he's watching the Tanners screw in their fuck dungeon. He blushes and smiles a bashful smile when he opens his eyes. "They're interesting. Nobody knows about the fuck room, though. Darryl even did his own framing and drywall."

"I have to see this."

"We can't. I have gifts to deliver." He points to the front door.

"I know that, but we can slow time down a little, right? There's no way I can leave this house without seeing a real-life sex dungeon."

His eyes darken, and I know what he's thinking. I'm thinking it too. How will I stand in a sex dungeon without touching him? I'm playing with fire if I let him lead me into the Tanner sex dungeon and do something. Would he tie me up? Spank me? Do they have whips and floggers? Cuffs and ropes? Somehow, the idea of him touching me in their sex room turns me on like I haven't been laid in years. My already uncomfortable tights suddenly feel wetter and downright stifling, like they're choking my legs. My bra tightens as my nipples push against it. Something visceral happens to my core as my stomach burns and clenches with something akin to nerves.

Probably nerves.

God damn me to hell, but I want this man's hands on me. I want his mouth on me. I'd let him tie me up or tie me down. I don't care. I want to see a real sex dungeon, and if he makes a move on me while we're in there, I'll go with it. He could do whatever he wants. He's intoxicating.

Without thinking, my hand touches his leg. He startles but doesn't pull away. He stares at my hand a second, then covers it with his own warm hand, trailing his thumb up to my wrist. His fingers are masculine and hard against my soft skin.

He inhales deeply. "A few minutes can't hurt, right?

"Come on," I say, getting up from my seat. I grab the same hand that was just touching me and pull him to what I hope is the door leading to the basement. "We'll be out in two shakes."

I guess correctly with the door, and Jasper's boots are heavy on the wooden basement stairs behind me. When we reach the bottom of the stairs, I put my hands on my hips and look around, confused. There's a den and what looks like a storage area, but I don't see anything like a sex room. "Where is it?"

"It's behind some stuff in the storage room," Jasper says, walking in front of me. He pulls a string in the storage area, and a bare lightbulb blinks to life. "It's in there."

I follow where he points and gasp when I see a little outline of a door. It's something even a plumber or electrician would miss if they did work down here. It's a small cutout of drywall that looks like someone replaced the drywall and didn't do a very good job. Jasper walks to it and pushes his fingers around the cracks until he gets a good grip on it and pulls the door away from the wall. "After you," he says, waving me into a hidden room about the size of my living room and flicking the wall switch for the lights.

I blink a few times and stare. I don't know what I imagined, but it wasn't...this.

A full-size disco ball hangs from the ceiling. The walls are red, and neon lights of purple, red, white, pink, and blue point at the disco ball. I squint from the flashing lights around the room and look away at the furniture until I get used to the strobe-like effect. The fact this is someone's suburban basement and not a Berlin discotheque is surreal.

There's a queen bed under the disco ball and mirrors surround the bed on three sides. Against the wall is something that looks like a wide workout bench but I'm pretty sure isn't used for lifting weights. A nearby wall hosts floggers, a whip, and all manner of restraints, including handcuffs. There's even a ball gag. "Who wears this?" I ask myself, not really expecting Jasper to answer.

"Darryl when he plays bottom."

"You know, it's going to take a long time for me to get used to you knowing that stuff."

"Sorry. I'll try not to freak you out even more than you probably already are." He picks up a nearby remote that was lying on the bench. "What do you think this does?"

"No telling."

He flicks the remote, and the lights dim. It's a welcome relief. Only the purple track light shines against the disco ball now. Jasper presses a couple more buttons and soft music comes through hidden speakers in the wall.

I turn in a circle and spin right into Jasper's arms. "Care to dance?" he asks, whisking me around the room to the soft music as I laugh.

"This is not exactly what I thought it would be."

"What did you envision?" he asks.

"A rack like in old dungeons. Maybe one of those tie-down tables you see in horror movies."

"Nope. You get disco balls and fuzzy handcuffs. I like to think the disco ball was Kristin's touch."

He pulls me closer and my breath hitches. Slowly, I raise my eyes to look at him. His eyes are hooded and dark. His jaw is clenched, and I feel something else throb against me through the Santa suit. "You got to see the sex dungeon. Is there anything...well, is there anything you want to try while we're here?"

I sputter, and it comes out like a cough. "Jasper, are you asking if you can whip me?"

He grimaces. "I don't know about that, Holly. I'm worried I'd hurt you since I'm not exactly trained in knot tying and proper flogging technique."

"I think the pain is kind of the point."

"I don't know about hurting you. Is there..." His voice trails away, and he takes a deep breath. "Is there anything I can do to make you feel good while we're here? Maybe have fun with one of the toys?"

"What did you have in mind?" I ask, my voice shaking. My nipples are at attention, and my entire body hums with want. I grip the woolly fabric of his Santa suit and flex my fingers.

He leans his face next to my jaw, enough that I can feel the sandpaper of his beard scruff. "I could put you on that bench over there and return the favor from this afternoon."

"You paid good money for that hand job. Do I have to pay you?" I ask, teasing.

"No, ma'am. I'll touch you for free. Consider it payment for a job well done tonight." He runs his nose up my jaw and places a small kiss on my earlobe. The movement practically brings me to my knees. My clit throbs. "I want to make you feel as good as you made me feel today. Would you like that?"

A whimper escapes my mouth, and I freeze with nerves. Thankfully, Jasper takes control and walks us to the bench behind me. He lays me back and never breaks eye contact. He doesn't blink, and I try to match his stare. He bites his lip and breathes through his nose in a rhythm I try to match as he gently pushes me back until I'm looking at Darryl and Kristin's ceiling. The purple lights scatter across the room, and I gasp as Jasper kneels before me and lifts both my legs into the air. He sets them both on his left shoulder and places a kiss on my knee through my tights.

"May I take off your tights, Holly?" he asks, his voice husky.

"Yes," I whimper, not recognizing my voice.

I kick my shoes off before he can do anything, and they land with two separate plops on the floor behind him. I urgently want this man to touch me, and the old sneakers are a hindrance. He slides his hand under my skirt and hooks his fingers in my tights. He inhales through his nose as he slides the tights down my legs inch by inch until he throws them over his shoulder with a chuckle. "Panties next?"

"Please," I beg.

He does the same thing to my panties except he doesn't throw my lacy underthings behind him. He balls them in his fist, meets my eyes, and pushes them to his nose, sniffing deeply. "Fuck, Holly. I've been wanting to know what these panties smell like all day."

"They're dirty. I've worn them since this morning."

"Yes, you have, sweetheart. If they were clean and detergent fresh, I'd be disappointed."

My mouth is dry, and I'm speechless. What does a girl say to a guy that thinks her dirty panties are delectable?

Thankfully, I don't have to answer. I watch open-mouthed as he sniffs my panties again like there's a line of cocaine in the crotch, finds the gusset, and sticks the fabric in his mouth, sucking on it as his eyes flutter.

Fucking Christ, I've never seen a man try to eat my underwear. Why do I like it so much? Here's a man kneeling before me and sucking the juice out of my panties, and it looks like he's eating cheesecake. My fingers itch for something of his to grab. Dick. Balls. Whatever. Let me at it. I sigh as he takes the panties out of his mouth a moment later, bunches them up again, and shoves them into his pants pocket.

He gently takes my legs off his shoulder and runs a hand down my calf, my knee, and thigh. "Spread your legs for me. Let me see you. All of you."

I obey. There's nothing that could make me stop. I open my legs, unashamed. I'm such a brazen slut for him that I even lift my skirt above my waist and let him look at every inch of me. My thighs. A few dots of cellulite on my hips form as I spread my legs wide, straddling the bench. I simply don't fucking care. I don't worry that I haven't shaved the old beaver for a few days. If he minds the stubble, he doesn't mention it. He doesn't look like a man picking apart every flaw of my center. He looks like a hungry man that's been presented with a turkey dinner.

He licks his lips and groans a little as his finger starts at my waistband and travels straight down my slit. I shiver as the digit passes my clit and dips into my pussy. He pulls his finger back like my cunt is too hot to stand but immediately sticks his finger in his mouth and closes his eyes like he's tasting birthday cake.

"Fuck, Holly. I was just going to use my hand like you did for me today, but you taste so fucking good." He gestures to my throbbing slit and sticks his tongue out of his mouth just enough to bite the tip of it. "May I?"

I give a small nod, my own body betraying me by its lack of communication. That tongue. Just looking at it right there between his white teeth does something to me.

He leans forward and places a small kiss on my abdomen. He looks up at me with wide eyes and slides down my body, slowly placing kisses on my bikini line and the top of my slit. I shiver when he gets there, and I tremble harder when he slides his middle finger inside my pussy. I arch into him as his tongue flicks out and catches my clit with the tip.

I'm on fire. I'm going to burn here and go to hell and burn there for letting Santa's son eat my pussy in someone's sex dungeon. But I can't stop. I won't. I grip his hair and pull him closer to me. He chuckles at my arousal and exuberance. He laps at me like a kitten eating cream, and I buck wildly against his face. Will he go home and tell the elves about the wild tugger from Pennsylvania that fucked his face without shame?

Fuck, I hope so. Because I won't forget any of this.

Jasper's tongue tests me, tasting me with light strokes. Once he's used to me or sure I'm not going to kick him away, he hums against my clit and pulls my legs over his shoulders. I wrap them at the ankle and close my eyes as Jasper licks, sucks, and kisses every single inch of me down there. He tongues my pussy and moves back to my clit, but when his tongue is in my pussy, he nuzzles my clit in clockwise circles with his nose. When he's tasted enough of my pussy, he slides back and licks my clit in long licks, moaning while he does it. A hand wanders up my torso and palms my breast under my shirt.

I push up to my elbows, insistent that I'm going to watch all of this. I want to see every lick. Every tongue fuck. I want to see my wetness on his fingers after they've been inside of me, and I want to see his facial expressions as he does it.

He smiles at me. "You like watching?"

"Yes," I whisper. I don't recognize my voice because it shakes as my orgasm builds behind my belly button.

He must feel my stomach contracting and notice the desperate way I paw at his hair. My vision blurs, and I throw my head back on the padded bench. There will be no watching for me as my eyes flutter closed no matter how hard I try to keep them open. When I do manage to catch a glimpse of his face, the only one watching anything is Jasper.

He watches every muscle tic in my face. He watches my breasts jiggle a little in my shirt as I curl into a crunch position from the force of the orgasm as it rips through me. He watches my mouth moan for him. He doesn't blink as I run my feet and legs over his back and shoulders.

I tremble as electric pleasure moves up and down my spine, down to my toes that flex against his magic suit, and up to my tongue that flops around in my lolling mouth. He licks, sucks, and nose nuzzles me until I stop shaking and moaning something that sounds like his name.

When I can lean up on my elbows again, he smiles from between my legs, takes one long lick up my slit, and places a last kiss on my belly button. "Are we even now, Holly Hepperdine?"

"Oh, Mr. Nicholas, I'd say I actually owe you after that."

His fingers trace my hips and thighs. "That's how good you made me feel today. It was wild how hard I came from just your hand."

"I want more," I whisper. I don't know where the desire comes from. The man just finished me.

He grins a sly grin. "What exactly do you want?"

"Something. Anything." I grip the collar of the suit and pull him up to me.

He settles on top of me and strokes my hair back from my face. I must look a fright. My hair is probably everywhere. If I look half as rumpled as him, I'm a mess. His hair sticks out in several places, and wetness glistens on his beard scruff. He lowers his mouth to mine so that I taste him on my tongue.

"Take this suit off, Jasper. I want your skin on me."

He unbuttons the suit and throws it across the room like he's a stripper throwing the suit to the crowd. The fabric hits the wall and slides down behind a cabinet. He leans up so I can run my hands down his chest.

Dear Lord, his pecs are cut. His abs are so sculpted, I could wash my clothes on them. Seeing them in the parlor today under the crappy lighting didn't do them justice. "Holy shit," I mutter.

"What do you want, Holly? You need to tell me."

"I want you inside of me. Do you have a condom by chance? Please tell me you have something. Condom. Rubber glove. Something."

He pulls back. "Fuck. I don't." He slides off me and goes to the nearby nightstand. Opening the drawer, he cringes and searches through odds and ends. "No condoms. They have everything else you could ever use with a dick. No condoms, though. Want me to pull out?"

I shake my head. "I'm mid-cycle. Not a good time to play roulette. I don't want a soldier to slip by the goalie." I groan and flop back on the bench. Fuck, I want him inside of me. Something needs to get inside of me. After the most intense orgasm of my life, I want to be fucked. I want to be fucked hard.

"Uh, Holly, if you want some fun, we can still have fun."

"I'm not using their sex toys," I say, nodding to the still-open drawer. "Gross."

"Because they've been used?"

"You don't know if they clean them properly."

"Well..." His voice trails off and he smooshes his lips together like he's humming.

"Well, what?"

Jasper pulls out the package for the Tanners that is still in the large pockets of his pants and holds it up. "We could use these. They're fresh."

Chapter 8

HOLLY

"**A**re you insane? We can't unwrap and use their sex toys."

"Why not?" Jasper asks, but his voice is different. Manic. I don't recognize his voice or the look in his eyes.

Is he as desperate for me as I am for him? Does he burn for me to have my hands on him like he just did for me? My tongue and lips? My mouth waters at the thought of that gorgeous dick in my mouth.

"What happens if they wonder why they didn't get a Santa gift this year? And what are we going to do? Have the reindeer fly low and throw Kristin's dildo into a dumpster when we're done with it?"

Jasper huffs and unwraps Darryl's gift, holding it up for me. "Ever use one of these?"

I stare at the package for a moment, my thoughts blank. Oh. My. God. "I give hand jobs. I'm not what you'd call an anal bead connoisseur."

Jasper smiles. "I'd be down for it."

I squint. "When you say you'd be down for it, do you mean you'd be down for me using it on you?"

"Sure. Why not? We're in a sex dungeon, and you wanted to check it out. I can't expect you to try something if I'm not down with it first." Jasper opens the package and pulls out the anal bead wand, which is the newer style and not the old clacker balls of yesteryear. It looks like a beaded dildo with smaller lumps at the tip of the wand that get larger toward the handle. The handle is circular with a hole in it. Do I put my finger through that loop or something?

"I've never done this before. What if I hurt you?"

Jasper walks over to the bench and drops his pants like he's at the doctor's office for a standard procedure. He leaves his boots on because they're laced up high. Luckily, his ankle hems are elastic, so he pulls the pants around his boots. He quickly kicks off his suit pants, picks them up, and throws them to the other side of the room where they land in what looks like a pile of dress-up clothing that's used for BDSM. I'm so used to men pulling down their pants at my job, that I ignore his hard dick as it weeps for me and stare at the blue anal bead wand Jasper waves in his hand. "With this? How would you hurt me?"

"What if I shove it in too far?"

Jasper goes back to the nightstand. He opens the top drawer and pulls out a bottle of lube. "You can use this."

"Once it's in, do I just pull on it until it pops out?"

"Do you think it's like starting a lawn mower?" he asks, and I can't tell if he's joking. His voice is deadpan. Serious. If he's joking, he has a very dry sense of humor.

"I'm pretty sure I don't pull it out like starting a lawn mower. I should pull it out slower than that."

"Well, it's a good thing you're trying it on me first because I'd probably get so excited if I was doing it to you that I'd pull it out like starting a lawn mower."

"Definitely not going anywhere near my ass with that thing until we figure this out, Jasper."

"Do you want to Google it?" he asks, nodding. "We should research it so we know for sure."

I feel around the pockets of my skirt and pull out my phone. "How to use anal beads. Christ on a cracker, I can't believe I'm searching this."

Several options come up on the home screen. I click one and quickly read through it while Jasper reads over my shoulder like we're simply perusing a restaurant menu. "This looks easy enough," I say. "I just pull it out slowly. It says it can be amazing."

He kisses my neck and nuzzles my ear. "I have other ideas, you know?"

"What kind of ideas?" I giggle. I put my phone back in my skirt pocket and reach up until my hand is in his hair again. "Good ideas?"

"I want your mouth on me while you use the toy."

"Fuck, Jasper. You're filthy."

"Oh, you have no idea, Holly Hepperdine. I'm not done yet. You said something about wanting something inside of you. How about you get the best of both worlds? You suck me off and use the anal beads on me. Kristin's new dildo has a suction thing on it. Let's stick that bastard on the wall. I want to watch you fuck it while you blow me."

"Holy hell."

"You down for it?" he asks, raising an eyebrow.

There is no way I'm saying no to being spit-roasted between Jasper and Kristin's brand-new dildo. After what he did with his mouth, he could suggest fucking me with a sledgehammer handle right now, and I'd clap.

I lean over and grab the dildo box again, open it, and slide out a blue nine-inch dildo. "They must really like blue, huh? Why is it bigger?"

"Probably because of the wall suction cup. You need more room to allow for your legs. You'll realistically only take around four of that, right?"

"I don't know." I shrug. "I've never fucked a wall dildo."

"That makes two of us."

Jasper grabs the dildo and stares at it for a minute like he's trying to figure out how this is going to work. "Awfully life-like." He looks around the room and walks to the wall behind the bench, licks the suction part of the dildo, and sticks it against the wall. We both inspect it for a moment until Jasper reaches forward and flicks it with his index finger, chuckling when the dildo wobbles like a door stopper but stays attached. "Seems sturdy. Get on, sweetheart."

"Does that line work on all the ladies? Get on?"

Turning to face me, he nudges me back against the wall and boxes me in with his arms. His biceps flex next to my face, and my fingers come up to the spot of chest hair between his pectorals. I run my fingers through the hair there and move up his neck.

"It never works. I have zero game. Just out of curiosity, is it working now?" he asks. His mouth dips down to mine, and I melt into him, letting his tongue explore my mouth like it just explored other places.

My hands slide down his abs and whisper over his erect cock. Wetness coats the tip of my finger, and I move my hands to his back, flexing my fingers as I massage him. I want to feel every muscle under his skin. Learn how he moves.

I break our kiss and place one small kiss at the corner of his mouth. My legs jiggle, and I swoon a little when a soft growl comes from his chest. His chest heaves as he catches his breath.

"You bet your ass it's working," I say.

His hand comes gently to my throat, and I cover it with my own hand, encouraging him to grip it harder. I've always been a sucker for a good hand on my throat during sex, and my heart skips a beat that he's willing to play dirty games.

"Get on, huh? It's that easy?" I ask.

He lets me go with a laugh and backs away from me. I miss the heat of his chest against mine, and the cool basement air makes the hair on my arms stand up. I almost moan for him to come back, but he's already turned away and is leaning over the dildo stuck to the wall.

"We can use the Tanner-provided lube, or I can just get this ready for you."

I don't answer or nod. It's a rhetorical question because I know he's going to personally get the cock ready for me to fuck.

My mouth drops open as he bends down, runs his tongue over the dildo, and flicks his tongue over the tip like he just did to my clit. He gives a devilish grin and takes the dildo entirely into his mouth like he's giving it a blow job, even bobbing his head a few times as I watch. Watching a guy take a dick into his mouth, even if it's fake, does things to me. Wobbly knees. Tunnel vision. Throbbing in places I haven't throbbed in for months.

He comes off it with a pop. "Here you go." He waves his hands over it like it's a prize on a game show. "All ready for you, sweetheart."

How could a girl say no?

I walk to the dildo and bend over, climbing onto the bench with a shimmy and lifting my skirt. I expect him to stand in front of me, dick in hand, waiting for his blow job, but he puts his hand on my back and eases me onto the toy, watching every inch of silicone slide into me as far as I can go.

I circle my hips to get used to the girth and length as Jasper runs his hand up my back. He lifts my shirt and unhooks my bra so that the cold basement air hits my nipples. He palms my breasts and moves with me as I glide forward and back, fucking the toy. His wet, warm spit on it makes it more lifelike, and I close my eyes, getting into a rhythm as I push myself against it.

"Used to it now?"

I nod, and he moves in front of me. I don't hesitate or waste time. Gripping his cock, I slide my tongue over his dick and flick my tongue over the hole. His salty taste hits my tongue, and I wrap my lips around the head of his cock, drawing the wetness off him. He runs his hands through my hair and purrs. He actually purrs. Dear fuck, did I make a man lose his mind so much that he became an animal?

I want to know if I can make him lose his fucking mind.

I dip down and take as much of him as I can, gagging and coughing when I back off him. He flexes his butt muscles and pushes forward as I move back like he's searching for me, wanting more. "Fuck, Holly, that feels so good."

Picking up the anal bead wand, I remove Jasper's dick from my mouth and replace it with the anal bead wand, looking at Jasper while I blow the toy. "Just want to get it wet for you."

He nods and inhales sharply. I've left him speechless as he watches me lube the toy with my mouth. He widens his stance and bites his lip when I take the wand out of my mouth and place it at the entrance to his asshole. "You sure about this?"

"Fuck yes. Turn on the vibration."

I flick the switch. "If it gets scary, pull my bangs. Not too rough. Just enough to know you're uncomfortable."

He nods again and squeezes his eyes shut as I inch the softly vibrating toy into his asshole. He startles at first, even though he was expecting it. His eyes open wide, and he takes a deep breath, breathing through the intrusion. "Gentler. I'm a little nervous," he chuckles.

I slow down and only press the anal bead wand into him bead by bead. He arches his back and pulls my head to his dick again. "Suck me to take my mind off of it."

I obey. I've always blown guys using at least one hand, but I can't this time or I'll fall. One hand holds the anal bead wand, gently moving it back and forth in Jasper's asshole. The other props me into doggy-style position against the toy stuck to the wall.

"Fuck the dildo, Holly. I want to watch you." Jasper's voice is husky and so damn masculine. Demanding.

I gently push back and take control of my own need for pleasure.

"Good girl, taking that dick while I watch," he whispers, wrapping his hands in my hair and bucking gently into my face.

It's hard to focus with the dildo inside me and his words driving me over the edge. I sputter and slurp around his cock. Fuck, I'd love to give him a leisurely blow job on the couch some night while we watch a movie. Concentrating on sucking his dick, working the beads, and fucking Kristin's dildo is both a physical workout and mental gymnastics. I don't know how porn stars do it.

I look up at him with wide eyes. There's something wild and unhinged about him. He doesn't care if I'm more slobber than suck on his dick as I struggle with keeping it in my mouth. His jaw flexes, and I know I may not be a porn star, but I'm *his* porn star right now. I've always been told men are visual creatures, and I'm driving him absolutely bananas.

My breasts swing wildly below me, and he cranes his neck to the side to take a look, licking his lips at the sight. "Fuck, Holly. You're so gorgeous."

I push the anal bead wand in further until my finger around the handle meets skin and he tugs on my hair with our signal. I slowly pull the wand out inch by inch, watching as he throws his head back and squeaks as each nub rubs his hole on the way out. His thighs squirm around the vibration in his ass, and when I have the tip out again, I gently push it back in.

"Leave it for a second," he gasps. "Just there."

The vibration must be hitting his prostate just right. He widens his shaking legs, struggling to hold himself up. I don't know how he's managed to stand through this. It can't be easy on his thighs to hold the wide stance.

I leave the wand for a moment as his stomach clenches in front of my eyes, curling forward in waves. I pull the anal bead wand out slowly again. This time, Jasper throws his head back and moans with each bead as it comes out of his ass. "Holly," he grunts. "I'm so getting one of these."

I'm so turned on by the mess I'm making of him that the dildo slides out of my pussy. I quickly get back on and fuck myself so hard I'll need aftercare from myself tomorrow. I don't usually come from penetration alone, but watching Jasper is doing things to me and pushing me to a type of orgasm I've never experienced. I now know why inexperienced men can see a woman's breasts and orgasm. Watching someone let go has never been so arousing. It's intoxicating, and my body hums with both pride that I'm doing this to him and amazement at how much I enjoy doing this for myself.

Jasper's entire body shakes as he holds back his release. I take one last pull on his cock and look up at him, sliding the anal bead wand back into his ass and letting him enjoy the feel on his prostate. "It's OK to come when you feel like it, Jasper," I whisper. "You've already impressed me enough for the night. If you want to come, come. I'll take it. I'll take every drop any way you want to give it to me."

"Yeah?" he coos above me. "Take it in your mouth and show it to me before you swallow."

I take his cock back into my mouth, and my cheeks hollow as I take long pulls. I'm so engrossed in the dildo and sucking him off that I hold the wand in his ass until it hits me that I should move it again.

As soon as the first bead comes out of his ass, he grips my hair and bucks into my mouth so far that I gag on the head of his dick. "Fuck!" he grunts before shaking and releasing into my mouth.

I choke on the cum as it coats my throat, but I manage to hold some in my mouth. When every drop is out of him, I come off his dick and open my mouth for him.

I'm not sure if he can even see right now, but he taps me under my chin with his finger, silently telling me to close it and swallow. I do it as I look at him, reveling in the feel of the warm liquid as it slides down my throat. I even make a show of gulping loudly as the last drop leaves my mouth.

Not really the last drop. One lone straggler sits in the corner of my mouth, and I swipe it with my finger before putting it in my mouth and sucking.

He moves to get off the bench, and he takes the anal bead wand out of my hand before coming to watch me with the dildo. "Do you have one more orgasm in you, Holly?"

"I don't usually come from penetration. It feels...full, but I'm not sure if I can come."

"I guess I need to help, huh?" he asks with a smirk.

Reaching under me, his finger hits my clit, and I jolt with both surprise and pleasure as it moves from my clit to somewhere at the base of my spine. He rubs my clit clockwise in three circles. That's all it takes.

Three.

Three measly times around my bundle of nerves.

The room spins again, and Jasper puts his other arm around my waist to keep me from collapsing onto the bench. "There it is," he whispers. "There's what you deserve."

My entire body shakes, and I lose all strength in my arm that's propping me up. I'm thankful Jasper holds me through my orgasm, cooing and shushing me. He congratulates me for a very human accomplishment with his words and touch.

When I'm spent, he gently lets me go, and I slink to the bench, the dildo still inside of me. I can only imagine how I look – hair a wreck and a wall dildo still inside of me as I'm bent over in yoga child's pose.

I simply don't care. Even more important, I don't think Jasper gives a shit.

He doesn't give a shit because the sound of footsteps on the floor above us makes us both freeze and suck in our breath.

Chapter 9

JASPER

We freeze at first. Holly's eyes widen, but she doesn't move from the dildo. She stays on it like she's trying to decide if staying on it and staying very quiet will keep the Tanners from finding us. I tiptoe back from the bench and put my finger to my lips. I point at the ceiling like I'm alerting her to intruders, and she gives me a dirty look. Obviously, she knows the Tanners are home.

I panic and start to sweat more than I already was, a nervous sweat replacing the sex glisten. I have no idea what to do. Make a run for it? Hide? Holly and I both look around the room. We don't discuss it, but she's obviously having the same thoughts about looking for a hiding spot.

Too bad there's nowhere to hide.

Holly moves first and slides off the dildo that glistens after she leaves it. I want to bend down and suck on it again, but licking the used toy clean would take time we don't have right now. Another time.

"What do we do with the toys?" Holly hisses, searching frantically for her tights.

Where the fuck did I throw her tights? And where the fuck are *my* pants and suit jacket? My mind spins, trying to assess the danger of getting caught and trying to remember where the hell I threw all of our clothes.

"Grab the toys and tuck them in your underwear."

"I can't find my underwear! You sucked on my panties and then put them in your pants."

We both frantically look around the room as Holly shoves the toys into the waistband of her skirt. Hopefully, the elastic will hold them there.

My suit! I need my suit. I can't get through the night without it. My jacket fell behind the cabinet, and my pants fell...

Holly pulls on my arm. "Jasper, someone's coming. We have to move. Now! Forget my panties. I don't wear them that often anyway. It's surprising I did today."

"I need my suit. I can't deliver the presents without it!"

She spins me around and gives me a push to get me moving, and I have no idea where she wants me to go. She spins me so that I face the other wall and not the door. She's panicking and probably wants me to simply move in one direction, either to find my clothes or get the fuck out. "You're not going to be able to deliver when you're beat up because Darryl found you naked in the basement. We need to go out the sliding glass entrance. Now!"

Holly's face is flushed with fear, and her hair resembles a bird's nest. Mascara pools under her eyes, and she's pulled down her shirt, not even bothering to hook her bra. I stare at her still-hard nipples through the fabric until she claps her hands in front of my face. "Jasper, now!"

Clothes. I need something to cover me. I can't run through the house naked.

I sprint to the BDSM costume bin and grab for my pants, not looking as I take off at a run and follow Holly through the cutout drywall, out the sliding glass door, and into the backyard. Holly glances up at the living room light once we're outside, breathes out a sigh of relief, and heads for the fence. The gate has a lock on it, and she curses before sticking her foot on a board and heaving herself over the fence, landing with a thump on the other side.

"I just wanted to have some nog and watch *Supernatural*. This is not how I thought this night would go," she mumbles, clapping dirt off her hands.

I follow Holly over the fence, and we run to the sleigh as fast as we can in the shin-deep snow. Thankfully, I never took my boots off, so my toes aren't freezing. Holly had the foresight to shove her feet into her Converse that were right next to the bench, so at least her toes won't fall off from the cold.

Our bodies are a different issue. Holly left without her tights, and I look at the back of her reddening bare legs, wishing I could make sweatpants appear out of thin air for her. I have my own frostbite problem since I'm totally naked in the moonlight except for my boots.

Holly turns to look at me for the first time since we left the house. "Jasper, you're naked! You didn't find any part of your suit?"

"I have my pants," I say, holding up the item I grabbed from the costume bin.

Holly's eyes widen before mine do. I should have felt a difference, but I didn't examine the fabric in my haste to get Holly and get the hell out of the house. I didn't think in my blind panic.

I'm holding assless chaps.

"Holy fucking shit! Where are your pants?"

"I must have grabbed the wrong thing!" I reply, looking longingly back at the house just visible through a thin spot in the trees. "Fuck! What the absolute hell?"

"You can't wear those to make deliveries."

I put my hands on my hips and look up at the moon, frustration squeezing my chest and almost hurting as much as the cold air literally freezing my dick off. "I can't make deliveries at all without my suit. At least not more than a handful tonight without being able to slow time. I also can't get into most houses unless the door is unlocked or a window's wide open. Not likely in December."

"We'll have to go back and get it," she says under her breath. "We're going to have to break into the sex room...again."

I nod and close my eyes. "I'll do it. There is no 'we' here," I say, making the apostrophe marks with my finger. "I can't risk you getting caught too. You're the only person that can help me if I get caught."

"I'm not letting you do this yourself."

"Yes, you will. I need you to stay with the sleigh and take it back home for me if something happens. The reindeer know the way in an emergency. Just take it home and tell my mother I'm a royal fuckup. She'll figure something out."

Her hand runs down my back, and she pushes her face into my skin before wrapping her arms around me from behind. "You're not a fuck up, Jasper. For what it's worth, this night has been an adventure."

I snort out a laugh. "Yeah, an adventure. I got you tased, and you're out here without leg coverings."

"There's a blanket in the sleigh. I'll be fine. Let's think about how to get out of this pickle."

I turn to her and don't even bother covering my dick. She looks down and raises her eyebrows. I follow her eyes and cringe a little. "Uh, yeah. I guess I'm happy you've already seen what it looks like normally. If you only saw it in twenty-degree weather, that'd be embarrassing."

A smile threatens the side of her mouth, and she stomps toward the sleigh. "What are you doing?" I ask.

"You can't walk around with nothing but assless chaps, Jasper. We need to find you something to wear until we get your suit back."

"All of the gifts in the sleigh are spoken for," I say, walking behind her.

"That didn't stop us from using the Tanner toys."

"That's different."

"How?" she asks. "Those were sex toys and one went in your asshole. How is borrowing someone's sweatpants not OK?"

"Because there are none in there that will fit me."

Holly stops with her legs dangling over the back of the sleigh. "Not one adult asked for clothes?"

I shake my head. "The Tanners are some of the only adults that still believe and write us. There are a few others, but if they ask for clothing, it's mostly socks or women's lingerie."

She bites her lip and then dives down into the decoy gifts to get to the warehouse. I have no idea what she thinks she's going to find. It's not like I can duct tape a bunch of socks together and go about the night.

I get into the sleigh and wrap a blanket around my body before sitting on the freezing bench. All I need is to get stuck to the freezing plastic and have Holly pour hot water on my ass to unstick me. That would be the cherry on top of this night.

Prancer turns around and huffs at me, blowing breath steam into the air. She shakes her head like she wants out of her bridle, and I flip her off. "What are you looking at? Didn't you ever see Dad naked because he left his clothes in a house? Turn around!"

She brays at me once and turns around. Thankfully, the other reindeer face forward, probably embarrassed to know me.

"Here we are!" Holly says, popping her head up from the back of the sleigh and holding up a pair of bib overalls.

"What are those?"

She shrugs. "I thought you'd know. I remember seeing bibs hanging on a hook near one of the golf cart things when I was down there before. If they're not a gift, maybe the elves use them as work clothes or something?"

I take the bibs and step out of the sleigh to put them on. "This will work. Holly, you're a genius. Have I told you that tonight?"

"Once already, but I like hearing it."

I step into the bibs, lament the way the crotch seam rubs against my dick and balls, and gratefully buckle each side of the bibs over my shoulders.

"Now that you aren't flapping in the breeze, we need a solid plan."

"OK, let me think." I pinch my nose and squeeze my eyes closed, forcing my brain to kick to life.

Why am I still thinking about that amazing blow job?

"Well, think fast. We're behind a bunch of evergreen trees, but if the Tanners decide to use their dungeon, they're going to wonder why there's a discarded Santa suit in there. We also left the disco ball and lights on. If they go searching the grounds, they'll find a guy dressed like Uncle Jesse from *The Duke's of Hazzard*, and eight reindeer strapped to a magical sleigh. We need solutions."

She's right. I take a deep breath through my nose and pull her to me. I need her arms around me right now, and I need to hug someone. I'd even hug Prancer at this point. I feel so alone. So naked – and that has nothing to do with the fact that I'm naked under bib overalls.

I let her go and grab the assless chaps. Thankfully, they untie in the middle, becoming two separate leather pieces, and I slide the leather over my bare arms. The result is turning myself into a hillbilly bat. Holly frowns, and I shrug. "It's all I have right now."

"Fair enough. What's the plan?"

"Do you have any clothes at your house we can borrow?"

"I don't have anything that will fit you. You're almost a foot taller and about 50 more pounds of solid muscle."

"Let's go to the next house on the list. If I can't get in, we'll see if there's a window or something we can shimmy through. Let's make a few easy deliveries and give the Tanners time to go to bed. Hopefully, they drank a shit ton of liquor tonight and will be too drunk and tired to notice if we sneak back into their sex dungeon in an hour."

Holly nods and looks around the sleigh while I tap the tablet to access the list. A team player and ready to get the show on the road, Holly throws her leg over the back of the sleigh, ready to go into the warehouse for any gifts we need.

I tap a few times on my tablet and find a nearby house that's barely in Holly's county. We're getting further out into rural Pennsylvania where few people live. The Helmcamps live a couple miles away, don't have dogs, and they don't have neighbors. It'll be an easy house if I can get into a window or shimmy up a drainpipe.

I pick up the reins and make a giddy-up noise that Prancer ignores, choosing to kick her back heels and fart instead. Holly and I both wave the smell away without comment. Prancer may think she has one up on us, but we've been through more terrible things tonight. The other reindeer take off, pulling the obstinate Prancer along, and we're airborne in a few seconds as Holly looks in the back for the Helmcamp child's present.

Chapter 10

HOLLY

"Do you want me to stay in the sleigh this time?" I ask as Jasper parks the sleigh in a crop of trees. The Helmcamp house faces a wooded area, and it's the perfect cover for eight reindeer.

Please say I don't have to go in. I'm obviously better at running stock and minding the sleigh than I am at delivering. As God as my witness, I'll never even look in another person's medicine cabinet. Being in other people's houses is for the birds.

"I think that's a good idea if you watch the reindeer," Jasper says, jumping out of the sleigh and giving a sad look at the chimney on the house. He can't go in that way, so we hope the door is unlocked. A lot of rural folks still don't lock their doors. "We're two for two with you tonight. I don't want you getting tased or distracting me in a sex room again."

"No problem." I wrap the bench blanket around me and tuck it between my legs. It's cold out here without underwear on. "And nice try, blaming that sex dungeon on me. I think we're both to blame for that."

He places Tara Helmcamp's gift on the bench next to me and leans over. Tugging on the blanket around me, he pulls me closer to him until his mouth hovers an inch from mine. Why does his breath always smell like peppermint? I swish my tongue around in my mouth, hoping my breath doesn't taste or smell like burnt ass. When he plants a gentle kiss on my lips, he crinkles his eyes.

"I think I have bad breath."

"I don't care," Jasper says, shaking his head. "I want to kiss you with tongue."

I move my head to the side and kiss his cheek instead. "Better get going, or we'll have a problem in the sleigh. Every time you kiss me, I want to attack you."

"That's a bad thing?"

"We're in enough shit."

Jasper huffs, grabs the present, and turns to walk to the house fifty yards away. When he's halfway to the house, he looks back at me, smiling. "There are candy canes in the console, Holly. I expect to kiss you in a couple minutes when I get back." He makes finger guns at me. "I expect tongue."

I run my eyes up and down his body. Black boots. Dark denim bib overalls. Black leather chaps on his arms with the strings hanging down his biceps. The ridiculousness of the outfit finally hits me, and I cover my mouth with a giggle.

As ridiculous as he looks, I'd still fuck him.

Without waiting for him to get all the way to the house, I find a candy cane, unwrap it, and stick it in my mouth as I watch Jasper walk to the Helmcamp door, jiggle the knob, and slouch.

Shit. The door's locked.

Maybe he'll try a window.

Jasper must have the same idea because he steps over bushes that come up to his thighs and peeks in the window. From the size and position of the windows, it's probably the living room. He cups his hands and looks left and right. Stepping back, he looks up at the house, looks back at me, and points to the second story.

"No!" I hiss. He can't hear me from where he is, but I wave my hands. "Don't go up there."

He walks to the drainpipe at the side of the house and next to a climbable tree and pulls the pipe, testing to see if it's sturdy. When it doesn't come away from the siding, he gives me a thumbs up and acts oblivious to the fact that I'm standing in the sleigh and waving my hands.

"Come back here right now, Jasper!" I whisper, pointing to the ground.

He shakes his head and points at the tree next to the house like he's going to use the branches to work his way up the drainpipe. Is he insane?

But who's more insane? The crazy person or the person that follows the crazy person? Apparently, that's me tonight.

What's the universal signal to tell someone they're a moron? I rack my brain for a way to tell Jasper to not do it, but all I can do is wave my arms and silently kick at the snow in frustration.

Jasper ignores me, obviously focused on doing his job and desperate to get inside the house. He tucks Tara's gift in the front of his bibs and lifts himself up to the first limb, pulling his feet up and holding on like a sloth. A look of confusion crosses his face like he doesn't know what to do next. Maybe he didn't climb many trees as a child. Eventually, he pulls himself up until he can sit on the branch.

Jasper takes a deep breath and then reaches for the next limb, this time using his feet against the side of the house to push himself up. He does this branch by branch until he can get on top of the porch. He grabs the pipe and pulls himself onto the black shingles, turning and giving me a thumbs up. I shake my head back at him, and he ignores me.

He walks across the roof of the porch to the first window, looks in, shrugs, and tiptoes to the next one. He lifts the window, and it doesn't budge. So much for rural people leaving their doors and windows unlocked. The Helmcamp house is locked up tighter than a nun's knees.

Jasper stands on the roof with his hands on his hips and looks around. The attached garage is next to the porch, and Jasper studies at it for a moment. It would be a big jump to get to the sloped roof of the garage, and it's possible he could miss, roll off the roof, and then we'd be in a medical emergency pickle.

He crouches into a runner position, and I open my mouth to stop him just as a light goes on in the room Jasper's standing in front of. The sudden brightness startles him, and he reels back, waving his hands for balance.

I scream. I can't help it. It's a blood-curdling scream like in horror movies. I hear it and know it's my mouth making the noise, but I have no control over it. It just escapes, and I don't even cover my mouth.

My scream must startle him more, but he doesn't fall off the roof. Another light clicks on in the house – this one downstairs – as Jasper reaches out and grabs the aluminum drainpipe. Unfortunately, the drainpipe can't hold his weight and peels away from the house with a sickening scratching sound like nails on a chalkboard. Tara's present falls out of the front of his bibs and lands in a bush.

Jasper falls into the tree and dangles in the branches, kicking his legs. The door swings open, and a naked man with white chest hair comes out, a shotgun in his thick hands. "Freeze, pervy mother fucker!"

Jasper's eyes widen and he goes still, his mouth wide open like he wants to defend himself but can't think of how to do it. He's no match for a gun, and what can he say to explain why he's in bib overalls and assless chaps while sneaking around on this man's roof. What is the man supposed to think? Of course, he'll think Jasper is peeping or up to other shenanigans.

"If you run away before the cops get here, I'll pump you so full of lead, the EPA will quarantine your body," the man says, chewing his lip like it's a habit to chew a toothpick.

"Cops are on the way, Don," a woman says from the doorway. She's in a floral bathrobe and wraps another bathrobe around her husband. "You don't want to be naked when the sheriff gets here."

Jasper pulls himself so that the branch he's holding is under his armpits, but he doesn't move. He doesn't speak. He stares at the man with the gun on him.

Fear overtakes me, and I double over, dry heaving on a nearby bush. Nothing comes up since I haven't eaten in hours, but my stomach tightens. My throat burns with the effort. What the fuck do I do? Do I charge the guy with the gun and risk getting shot? Even if the man isn't a jerk, startling him while he's holding a gun is idiotic.

Minutes pass, and the man's wife brings him slippers to stand in and leans in the doorway watching Jasper dangle from a branch. This night can't get any worse.

Until it does...

A police car rolls up the rocky driveway, the crunch of the tires breaking the silence. The doors open and Officers Lyle and Coop slowly get out of the car. Coop adjusts his belt while Lyle talks into the radio on his shoulder, saying something I can't hear.

Lyle and Coop both come into the parlor on teambuilding days. I don't know much about their life situations since neither man wears a wedding ring when in the parlor, but Lyle's dick matches his build – short and stocky with a patch of graying pubic hair. Coop is tall and skinny with a pencil dick to match. Both guys are decent enough to my coworkers and me during their visits, but they're cold. Frigid. They don't talk much except to each other. They're the perfect police partners, able to communicate with each other by eye contact and facial expressions.

"What the heck?" Coop asks, strolling toward the tree and house, his hand on his taser.

Great. More tasers.

"What's going on, Don?" Lyle asks, approaching Mr. Helmcamp.

Mr. Helmcamp lowers his gun and nods at Jasper. "Some kind of freak sneaking around on the roof outside Tara's room. He may be a pervert."

Oh. Fuck. It's not enough that Jasper was caught. He was caught outside their daughter's room.

Lyle rubs his face and looks at Jasper. "You want to tell us why you're hanging in a tree and why you're sneaking around outside a little girl's room?"

Jasper must grasp the severity of the situation because he curses before groaning. "I'm going to drop down now. My arms are tired holding on to this branch. I won't run."

Coop nods and grunts in affirmation, and Jasper drops to the ground in a crouch position. He rises slowly, his hands in the air.

"What the fuck do you have on your arms?" Mr. Helmcamp asks.

"Are those chaps?" Lyle asks. Everyone turns in slow motion to look at him, probably wondering why he knows exactly what assless chaps look like when they're on someone's arms. Lyle shrugs and focuses on Jasper. "Why are you wearing chaps on your arms?"

"What kind of sick fuck are you?" Mrs. Helmcamp asks from the door.

"Answer the lady's question," Coop chimes in. "You know what? I don't care to hear your bullshit because there is nothing you can say that would make this OK. Get on the ground. Hands behind your head."

Jasper slowly drops to his knees and gets on the ground. He puts his hands behind his head as I helplessly watch Lyle approach him and run his hands over Jasper's body, searching for a weapon. Lyle handcuffs Jasper and pulls him up. "He ain't even wearing underwear," Lyle says with a sneer. "No t-shirt or anything. No underwear lines under these bibs."

"You sick, deviant piece of shit," Coop replies, shaking his head at Jasper. He grits his teeth and flexes his fists, and I see him flick something on his shoulder as Lyle does the same. Did they turn around their body cameras? "You're under arrest for trespassing and disorderly conduct because that's all I can get you on without you actually getting into the house, but we don't take kindly to perverts around these parts. I should let Don take care of it for all of society with that shotgun and tell everyone we got here too late. That's what I want to do to guys like you."

"It's not what you think," Jasper says. "I think I'm at the wrong house."

"You sure as shit are, son," Mr. Helmcamp says from the porch. "Take this piece of shit off my property."

Both officers nod at Mr. Helmcamp and turn Jasper toward the police car with its spinning red and blue lights. Lyle pushes Jasper toward the car, and I wince as Jasper almost trips over a rock.

When they reach the cruiser, Lyle puts his hands on Jasper's head and nudges him into the back of the police car. Jasper doesn't look in my direction, probably not wanting to draw attention to the fact that I'm hiding behind a tree. Jasper's as pale as a ghost, and his forehead wrinkles in concern for his sleigh, me, and the gifts that still need to be delivered. Maybe it's a combination of concern for all three.

Coop, always more observant, looks around the area like he knows he's being watched. He shines his flashlight beams around the area, squinting as he shines the light on the tree line. I straighten behind an oak tree, my arms straight at my side and thankful that the tree I picked to hide behind is wider than the others around it. There's no way Coop would miss a flouncy skirt if I was behind a smaller tree. Bark and twigs stick in my back, but I hold my breath and don't dare move.

Eventually, I stick my head around the tree trunk when I no longer see the flashlight beams across the foliage near me. Coop nods at Mr. Helmcamp, who still watches from the front porch in the old bathrobe, and gets in the car. I wait until Mr. Helmcamp goes back into the house and shuts the door before I take off at a sprint for the sleigh.

I'm going to have to drive it. Holy shit. I can't drive a sleigh pulled by eight reindeer. Jasper makes it look so easy to hold the reins. Is it like riding a horse? I rode a horse once at Girl Scout camp in seventh grade and used the reins to turn and stop the old nag. Something tells me driving eight reindeer is a different vibe.

I practically throw myself into the sleigh with a huff and move my unruly hair back from my face. Pushing my hands against my mouth,

I scream into my palm. The reindeer startle at the sound, and I throw my head back and look at the moon. "Fuck!" I yell, balling my fists. "Fuck fuck fuck fuck fuck fuckity fuck!" I swing my hands wildly like I'm punching the air.

I shouldn't panic, but I'm totally panicking.

Think, Holly. Do I get into the navigation system, punch in the coordinates for Jasper's home, and show up at his mother's door to explain that I gave her son a hand job today, fucked her angelic boy in a sex dungeon, and he then lost his suit and got arrested? Or do I go to my own home, park the reindeer at the nearby petting zoo, get in my jammies, and go to sleep? The last option is tempting, but I know Jasper would never leave me to rot in the county jail. Sure, I've only known him for a few hours, but I know a few things about him. For example, his dick tastes nice, he's a freak when you get him in a sex room, and he wouldn't leave me in jail. These are important things in a man and not something I'm likely to find on Tinder.

I have to go get him.

I bite my lip and look at the reindeer. "OK, ladies, new plan." Do they understand me? I should have asked Jasper if they're smarter than the average forest deer. "Some shit went down, and your dude is currently having mug shots taken. I'm going to go get him. So, I'm going to pick up those reins, but I've never driven a sleigh before. You'll have to give me some grace and help me out. That also applies to you, Prancer."

I glare at the obstinate animal, and she turns around again before kicking at the sleigh, flicking snow in my face.

"Fine. Be that way you sullen bitch. Blitzen!" I yell, hoping the reindeer at the front are more forgiving of a rural Pennsylvania girl just trying to bust her man out of the pen. "Get us airborne!"

I take the reins, snap them like I saw Jasper do, and give a small smile. There's a good chance this will be my only opportunity to ever do this. May as well do it right.

I call out each reindeer by name like the story that was read to me over and over as a child and hold on tight as the sleigh lifts into the air.

Chapter 11

JASPER

"Let me get this straight. You're Santa Claus's son," the man called Sheriff DeWitt says, typing my statement into his laptop.

I'm never going to live down being the only Santa to get caught, arrested, and fingerprinted. The elves will have a field day with this. My mother will be mortified. I'll be the laughingstock of rural Canada. Not that there's a lot of people up where I am, but the reindeer will be amused.

"Yes, sir. Last name is Nicholas."

"Tell me the story again. Slower this time. I don't type so fast."

Sheriff DeWitt smiles at someone behind me like I'm the butt of an inside joke. I know how crazy my life sounds, but he could be more professional.

Then again, it's hard to not knock all of his teeth out since I know he visits Holly. I glance around the police bullpen at the other man biting his lip to keep himself from laughing. All the men here visit

Holly, and I want to beat every single one of them to death with the chair I'm sitting on.

Have any of them ever asked that, instead of a hand job, they can put Holly in touch with services that will help with Helena's tuition? Point her to a food bank? Find her a prescription card that will help with her mother's medicine? Offer to be her clients if she wanted to start her own accounting service instead of being her hand job clients?

No. They let her jerk them off, knowing full well she's an accountant by trade. Like it's funny. So much for protecting and serving. Sounds like Holly's the only one serving anything in this county.

"I'm Santa's son," I start, taking a deep breath. I pinch my nose in frustration but keep going. As much as I hate them, they're in charge of my fate right now. I have to look like I'm calm and nice. "I met...a girl. We were in a house I was delivering to, and we, well, I lost my pants."

"How did you lose your pants?"

"I took them off so she could blow me while she used anal beads up my butt."

A laugh sputters behind me, and I glance back and glare at Deacon Messner right as he covers his mouth like he's fake coughing. The bastard was on the naughty list for the entire 80s and 90s. It's all I can do not to put his kids on the naughty list this year, even though they're not assholes like their father.

I turn back to Sheriff Dewitt. "The owners came home, and I had to leave without my magic suit."

"Right..."

"We were short on time, so I found some bib overalls in the sleigh and made the next delivery. I figured it was better than assless chaps. But since I didn't have my magic suit, I got caught in the yard. You guys showed up, and here we are."

Sheriff DeWitt clears his throat and rubs his forehead like I've given him a headache from hell. His forehead is wrinkled like I'd expect for a man of fifty-two. His frown turns down his mouth, highlighting the forming jowls on his face. His dark hair, what's left of it, is graying, and he pushes his wireframe glasses up his porous nose.

"Sir, I'm going to ask this one time. Have you taken anything tonight that may be altering your mental state?"

"Like drugs or something? No," I say, waving my hands in front of my face. "No drugs. No alcohol."

Sheriff DeWitt closes his laptop and rubs his face. "You're lucky we're not busy tonight. We don't usually put mental cases in general population."

"Mental case? I'm not mental! I'm telling the truth."

"Can anyone back up anything you're saying right now, son?"

Holly could back me up. I can't bring her into this, though. These men know her. I can't let them think less of her or think she's involved in this. If they find me guilty of breaking and entering, Holly could get in trouble. I hope she's far away from here. I hope she got on the sleigh and got to somewhere where she could use the tablet and call my mother for help. Surely, Holly would do that. She wouldn't just run away and abandon all the toys.

Abandon me.

This is a disaster. I look at the time on the wall clock above the sheriff's head and lament it's already after one in the morning in this time zone. I've got the magic touch with time, but only if I get my suit back. I have gifts to deliver, and this yahoo that likes hand jobs from my girl is holding me up.

"I have nobody that can back up my claim, sir. You'll simply just have to believe that you're keeping children from getting their gifts tonight. You're going to be sorry for this in the morning when children wake up and start crying."

"I'm sure. But I could just tell all their parents that Santy Claus should have been in his suit and not fucking around with a woman while wearing chaps on his arms like some kind of deranged bat. Something tells me that wouldn't go over well." He looks at Deacon and waves the younger deputy over. "Take Santa here to general population. He can sit with the drunk guy until he sleeps it off. If he's still adamant he's Santa tomorrow, call psych and have them pick him up." He moves a file to the side of his desk and takes a sip of coffee, grimacing at the taste or the temperature. "I'm too old for this shit."

It smells like pee in here. It could be the old, striped mattresses that look like they have more than pee stains on them, or it could be the smell has become ingrained in the floor after several years of drunk people peeing on the tile. I should have turned around and punched Deacon right in the face instead of letting him bring me to the den of piss.

At least I'm *almost* alone. Only one thing could make this night worse, and that's a prison fight and getting shanked or forced to blow some dude named Earl. The cells next to me are empty, and the two cells across the row from me are unused. One drunk man stands at the cell door three doors down and across from me. He's so drunk that his eyes droop and spit runs out of his mouth. He slurs something at me that I don't understand, resulting in more drool from his mouth, and I wave, deciding that staying as friendly as possible is my best bet. Maybe he'll be my new prison friend.

Turning away from him, I walk to the double-paneled windows and knock. Sturdy. I don't know why I thought they wouldn't be.

A human male couldn't squeeze through the small slot, but hopes of someone cutting me out through the window come to mind.

Nobody's coming for me, though. Not a soul in the world, save Holly and the douche canoes that work here, know that I'm here.

Who do I call for my phone call? My mother's in Canada. So are the elves. Dad's sick and completely incapacitated and doesn't even know who I am when I visit him. The only person I could call is Peter McQuiven, the man who has the Eagles season tickets next to mine. I only have his number because we take turns buying beer and hotdogs at games so only one of us needs to miss game action. I text him how many hotdogs I want one game. He texts how many beers he wants at the next. We sure don't have the type of relationship where we call each other to be bailed out of jail.

I don't cry often. In fact, I don't think I've cried since one of the elves tested a bowling ball by throwing it at my scrotum when we were fifteen. Tears come to my eyes now, though. My lids, not accustomed to salty tears on them, burn like I've never cried. It's such a foreign concept to my body. My hands shake, and I'm not sure what to do with them. I shove them in my bibs and shiver. It's cold in here, and the police took my arm chaps.

How did I fuck up so royally? I know. I wanted Holly and just wanted to enjoy her. Sweet, gorgeous Holly who's beautiful and smart enough to figure out Dad's stock system. It also doesn't hurt that her pussy tastes like butterscotch.

And that mouth.

She probably hates me. I've ruined Christmas for her forever. She won't be able to look at a mall Santa or even stockings for the rest of her life. Even worse, I ruined Christmas for kids around the world. Children are going to wake up to nothing tomorrow. Their stockings will be empty, not even a lump of coal in the toe. They'll think they've been naughty and react poorly, probably acting out in response. What's the point of being good for a year if Santa doesn't show up because he's getting railed by an angel with an anal bead wand? They won't write letters again, and our output will drop. Could my family lose their position? Would there be no Santa anymore? I'd actually have to get a job. It's not like I'm trained for anything. It's hard to believe, but there aren't a lot of practical, well-paying jobs for a guy whose only skills are testing toys and driving a team of reindeer.

Maybe Holly could get me a job at The Happy Stroke Club. I'd go from giving children gifts to jerking off grown men. My tips would be good since I'm a guy and know what I'm doing.

I plop on the stained mattress and put my head in my hands, letting the tear that was balancing on my eyelid drop to the floor. I stare at the stained tile and think. How can I ever fix any of this? Can I fix Christmas?

More importantly, can I find Holly and make all of this up to her?

Chapter 12

HOLLY

"Hi, Deacon," I coo, walking through the door. I wish I wasn't in sneakers. It's much easier to saunter or sashay in a sexy way with high heels on. "You're working awfully late tonight. Need some company?"

Deacon raises his head from where he's doing paperwork and startles, his light eyebrows rising to his dishwater blond hairline. He looks behind him like he's worried someone's watching, but the bullpen's mostly empty this time of night on Christmas Eve. Sheriff DeWitt's in his office pacing and on the phone with someone, smiling and probably wishing them a Merry Christmas. Beat cops are out doing their job. The only people here are Deacon, the receptionist at the front door, Sheriff DeWitt, and a younger guy I know from the massage parlor only as Roy. Roy, if that's his real name, stands in the back break area, stirring a cup of vending machine coffee and watching snow fall outside the window. He looks uneasy in his deputy uniform, and it sags a little in the thigh area.

"Holly Hepperdine?" Deacon whispers. "Are you OK? What are you doing here?" His eyes slide up my bare legs, and I shiver. It has nothing to do with the cold. Deacon likes a rough tug and can get a little handsy with my tits. "Did you get mugged or something and need to file a report?"

I sit in the bright yellow, plastic chair and cross my legs, smiling and tilting my head at Deacon like he has my full attention. Like he's a client and visiting the parlor. "Actually, Deacon, I was hoping you'd help me with something."

He smiles a toothy grin. Say what you will about the asshole, he looks nice. His brown eyes practically glow with the idea of helping the damsel in distress that jerks his cock when his wife won't pay attention to him. "I'd do anything to help you."

I point finger guns at him. "I'm glad to hear that, big guy." I don't even hide my inference that he has a big schlong. That's a total lie. He's the smallest dick I yank. "I need you to tell me if there's a guy here."

Deacon looks at Roy in the break area and leans back in his chair to catch a glimpse of Sheriff DeWitt still on the phone. "There are three of us here. If you want, I'm sure we could make your Christmas interesting. Bang bang, choo choo train, right?"

I giggle a girlish chuckle and tap his forearm, stroking it a little with my nails as I pull away. "No, silly. I was wondering if you brought another guy in. Bib overalls. Dark hair and a little stubble. Ring a bell?"

"The guy we picked up wearing assless chaps on his arms who thinks he's Santa?"

"Yes, that one," I nod.

"Friend of yours?"

"Kind of."

"Holly, let me give you some advice," he says, leaning in. I lean toward him, playing along. "Don't get involved with guys that think they're Santa. We had a guy think he was the tooth fairy once, and it wasn't pretty. If you need friendship, we're all more than happy to keep you company."

His hand slides over mine, and I look down at the gold watch on his wrist. I fucking hate this guy. I'd punch him in the face if I could. Most of my clients are normal guys, but this guy has a serial killer or power trip cop vibe and always has.

I pull my hand back and suddenly wish I could wash it. I only touch him with gloves on at work. This somehow feels more personal. Filthier. I smile and resist the urge to cringe at him. I don't care if he ever shows his face in the parlor again. I just need Jasper.

Get Jasper and get the fuck out so he can deliver the presents in his sleigh. That's the plan.

"Let's get down to brass tacks, Deacon. What can I do to get Jasper Nicholas out of the clink tonight besides paying tooth and nail in bail money we both know I don't have?"

Deacon's hand moves to his belt, and his fingers dance over the buckle. He looks behind him again. Luckily, Roy's realized I'm here and is on his way over to Deacon's desk. Deacon reddens and turns back to me with his lips in a grim line.

"Holly Happy Hands! How are you?" Roy says, walking up to the desk and slapping Deacon on the shoulder. "What brings you up here?"

Say what you want about Roy, I'd take him over a prick like Deacon any time. He's younger, around my age, and has no wife he cheats on when he comes into the parlor. He talks to me about monster truck shows and punk bands. He's actually a sweetheart. He asked me out once, and I turned him down because I don't like punk bands or monster trucks. I also didn't want a first date to be awkward because I was already familiar with his junk.

"I'm here to get the guy you brought in that thinks he's Santa Claus."

Roy and Deacon look at each other. "That guy?" Roy asks. "Don't tell me you're dating *that* guy."

Both men stare at me with slightly open mouths, and my hands clench so hard that I stick them under my legs so I won't show my anger. How dare these guys talk about Jasper like he's a drunk, a druggie, or a guy that cheats on his wife at a massage parlor? There are millions of worse men in the world, and Deacon is one of them. Roy's nice enough, but he shouldn't make fun of anyone.

"He's my friend," I say, a cool sound to my voice. "No boyfriend. What do you say, guys? Can I bust my friend out?"

Deacon laughs. "You know we can't just wave a magic wand and pop Santa Claus out of the clink, Holly. You have to pay bail."

"I don't have bail."

"Then you don't have your Santa Claus being held for disorderly conduct and trespassing."

Roy gives Deacon a side-eyed look before frowning and looking at me with kindness on his face. He may think Jasper's crazy, but he has the heart to feel a little bad about the situation.

I sigh and crinkle my face into a crying position. If I can work up some tears here, that'd be nice. OK, think of something awful. Horrible. Whale extinction. Global warming. Something, anything to work up some tears.

Even without real tears, Roy leans forward with a concerned look on his face and rubs my arm. Deacon reaches for a tissue, handing it to me and squinting like he's not sure I'm in need of comfort or trying to play on his emotional love for my hand jobs.

I take the tissue and wipe my eyes. "It's just...it's Christmas Eve, and Jasper was playing Santa for my little cousin. My cousin doesn't have much in life, you see. Her, uh, parents ran away and left her with our other aunt. She's parentless and was really looking forward to just one spot of joy in her life. Since she was three, all she wanted was to catch Santa on Christmas Eve as he was delivering presents." I sniffle and look up from the tissue, mostly to check if they're buying any of this bullshit. "We hired someone to play Santa so we could set it up so she could catch him. Jasper went to the wrong house and lost his suit. Then, he went to my cousin's old house by mistake. That's where you caught him. This is all a simple misunderstanding. Please, show mercy. If not for me, for poor...Sabrina. That's my cousin's name. Poor Sabrina, who has nothing in the world and just wanted to catch Santa."

Roy squats next to me and rubs my back just as Sheriff DeWitt comes out of his office and stops in the doorway, taking in the scene. "What in holy hell is going on in here? What is Holly Happy Hands doing here, and why is she crying?"

Deacon swivels around in his chair. "She's here to get the guy that thinks he's Santa Claus. She says she got him to pretend to be Santa so her little cousin could catch Santa on Christmas Eve."

I look up my tissue, dabbing my eyes like I'm Scarlett O'Hara. "He just got really into his character. He can't help it. He's a classically trained actor."

I have no idea where this bullshit is coming from before it spews from my mouth.

"Is that so?" Sheriff DeWitt asks, scratching his head.

"If you could find it in your heart to release him for tonight, I'll make sure he shows up to any court appearances and pays any fines." I put my hand over my heart and sniff again. "You have my word. Don't you all trust me?"

"Of course, we do," Roy soothes, still rubbing circles over my back.

Deacon picks up a pen and clicks it several times. "You need to pay bail for disorderly conduct and trespassing, Holly."

Fear sinks into my stomach. I have to get Jasper out of here. My only other option is to take the sleigh and deliver the presents myself.

Wait. Is that an option? I know how the stock works. I watched over Jasper's shoulder as he used the navigation tablet. Could I go back to the Tanner house, ring the doorbell, ask for the Santa suit I'd need, and just get on with the whole thing as the first female Santa to save the day?

Why the fuck not?

It's a last resort, though. I should *try* to help Jasper. He's amazing, handsome, kind, and all the things a girl wants in a man, wrapped up in a little red Christmas bow.

And that mouth.

I take a deep breath through my nose and increase the smile on my face until I'm sure the guys can see my back molars. "Alright, boys, whip 'em out."

Sheriff DeWitt startles and shakes his head. Roy pulls his hand off my back and tilts his head like I just took a shit on Deacon's desk. Deacon's hands move to his belt buckle, and he smiles like...well, like it's Christmas morning.

"Uh, Holly, that's not what we do here. This isn't the parlor," Sheriff DeWitt says. Deacon freezes with his belt buckle half undone, and a frown lines his face.

"I know that. Get out your parlor punch cards." I grab the hole puncher that's in Deacon's pen cup and click it a few times. "I'll initial above the top in case Linda One asks about it."

Roy's the first to let it sink in. He digs into the back of his pants, pulls out his wallet, and flips through it until he finds his punch card to The Happy Stroke Club. His hands shake when he hands it to me.

"Only three punches, Roy. I've seen you three times. You don't see any other therapist?"

"Only you, Holly. You have the magic touch. You're everyone's favorite girl."

"Isn't that sweet? That makes my heart sparkle like glitter." I smile and click his punch card seven more times and set the card on Deacon's desk so I can initial above each hole punch. I hand it back to him with a smile. "Here you go, honey."

"Thanks." He puts the punch card back in his wallet with a blush on his cheeks.

Sheriff DeWitt steps forward. "Well, this is the fourth card I've had. Just started a new one."

"Don't I know it, you dirty boy," I say, winking. "You see me quite a bit."

"Well, it gets me out of the house now that the arthritis is starting up. Bowling league isn't as much fun."

I take his card and punch the nine necessary spots to get him to ten and initial above the punches. Thankfully, Linda One doesn't keep great records and has no way to prove these guys aren't visiting this much. It's not like we want extensive customer files in case law enforcement outside of our small town wants to turn its eye on us. She definitely won't question Sheriff DeWitt. Even if he wasn't in law enforcement, I'm pretty sure the vast majority of our customers use fake names. I look at Roy out of the corner of my eye. He definitely doesn't look like a Roy. Is anyone under forty named Roy these days? Maybe I should have gone out on a date with him just to learn his real name.

I hand Sheriff Dewitt's card back to him, and he gives a little bow in thanks. He's never disrespectful when he comes to see me.

I look at Deacon as he thumbs through his own wallet. When he finds the punch card he needs, he pulls another two out with it. "Lyle and Coop gave me theirs to hold on to for them the last time we went. Punch theirs too."

I grind my teeth but maintain the smile. "Of course," I say, not moving my lips or blinking. I make a mental note to not tug Deacon as well as usual next time. No small talk or grins. Less lube. Fucker.

I punch all the cards as the men watch in silence, the only sounds in the room are the crackle of the scanner as a fire call for the fire department comes through and the sound of the hole punch. My hand is already tired from the hole punch, and I haven't even had to redeem the punch card sessions.

I slide the cards across the desk to Deacon, not wanting to risk our fingers touching if I hand them to him. He picks them up, squints, and counts the holes, mouthing as he counts to make sure I didn't stiff him or his buddies.

"Alright, Deacon, go let Santa out," Sheriff DeWitt says. He turns back to me and points his finger at me. "But he's got a court appearance for disorderly conduct at some point and will have to pay a fine. If he doesn't show or respond, I'm holding you accountable. Punch cards aren't going to pay the fine."

"Yes, sir."

My heart pounds in my chest. I can get Jasper! We'll go to the Tanner house and get his suit back. We'll get the presents delivered. Maybe I'll get to see him again on a normal night. Hell, maybe I'll get to spend a day with him during daylight hours outside of the parlor. Could I get to know him outside of Santa business and hand jobs?

"Hold on. That's it?" Deacon asks, throwing a pack of sticky notes he was holding onto his desk in irritation. "We're just going to release a guy because our favorite local hand hooker punches our punch cards?

She's just a sex worker. Why are we turning him over to her? Hell, we should at least take her in the back and have her suck our dicks if we're going to take bribes."

Don't throw up. Don't throw up.

It's not the suggestion of sucking his dick. It's the idea that I'm not a human to him. I'm a sex worker. The words rattle in my head like an echo. I have a degree. I have a family. I have a sister I take care of and a mother I'm the primary caregiver for. I pay the mortgage, the light bill, and the taxes. I shop at local restaurants and stores to support small businesses around me.

But I'm just a sex worker to him. OK, I'm a sex worker, but that's not all that I am. I'm a human that contributes to this man's society. Hell, this man kisses his wife on the cheek and comes to see me. Who, exactly, is the bad person in this situation? Who should receive the harsher judgment? It's not the woman that's trying to survive and never spoke wedding vows to anyone.

In our world, it'll always be people like me that are the bad guys, though. Even I know that, and I accepted it a long time ago.

Tears burn my eyes with the realization that the only person that's treated me like a human being and shown me any respect outside of my family is the man in the back cell that I came to get. And I'm going to get him, God dammit! No matter what I have to do and how unsavory it is.

I fold my hands in my lap and look at the toes of my Converse, waiting for Sheriff DeWitt to appease Deacon and tell him to take me in the back. I'll do it. So help me, I'll suck all of them off if it gets me Jasper.

"No, Deacon," Sheriff DeWitt says, and I lift my head so fast I almost get whiplash. "Just because we visit her business doesn't mean we coerce her to do something she doesn't want to do." He wags a crooked finger at Deacon. "You get your shit together and be a little more respectful. We all visit that parlor, but there are rules there. There are rules here, and you're going to follow them. Roy's going to follow them. I won't allow it." Sheriff DeWitt swings his eyes to me. "Get Holly a blanket. Her legs look cold. Roy, go get our Santa."

"We're just going to let a guy that thinks he's Santa out of the clink?" Deacon asks.

Sheriff DeWitt nails Deacon with a glare. "Did I misspeak?"

Deacon looks at the floor. "No, sir."

"That man was found in a tree. He wasn't upstairs in their teenage daughter's bedroom. He didn't break in. Hell, he could have been Christmas caroling while drunk. That isn't a death penalty offense. He went willingly and never showed violent tendencies. He's either drunk or needs mental care, and we've let people sleep it off here and release them before. He could think he's Pope Benedict and we wouldn't have a leg to stand on until he threatens someone. Go get him."

Deacon's chair squeaks when he stands. He pulls keys out of his pocket and walks away without a look or a word to anyone. Roy pats me on the back and walks back to the coffee station to watch more snow outside the window like a small child. I'm left with a visibly exhausted Sheriff DeWitt.

I should thank him. I should tell him I owe him more than a punch card. "Um, thanks. You didn't have to do that."

"What? Stick up for you when Deacon mouths off? That little shit stain – I'd throw him through a wall if I could. I've known you a long time, Holly. This whole town has. Sure, half the county visits you for hand jobs, but what you don't know is that a lot of them go to you or request you because they know you keep the lights on in that house." He turns to walk back to his office. He gets halfway and spins back around. "For what it's worth, I kind of hope to see the back of you someday."

"You want me to leave town? You think I'm that bad?"

He snorts. "No, honey. You're that good. I know it. We all know it. Even Deacon knows it deep in his balls. You deserve better than this piece of shit town. Listen to me. You get your momma and get the fuck out of here. Take her with you if you insist on caring for her."

He walks away before I can answer. I stand up to follow him and walk into his office to ask what ideas he has for how I could possibly manage to leave this town, but Deacon walks back into the room, Jasper tagging along behind him.

There's no protocol on how to act when your hookup springs you from jail on Christmas, but Jasper runs to me immediately, lifts me so that my legs dangle a few inches off the ground, and spins me around in a circle. Deacon makes a face like he can't believe I'm allowing Jasper to touch me.

Fuck that guy. Jasper can touch me any time he wants.

I laugh when Jasper stops spinning, and I slide down his body until I wrap my arms around him in a hug. I'd kiss him, but I just told the police that he wasn't my boyfriend.

I kick my legs, and he sets me down. "What are you doing here?" he asks, running his hand through my hair.

"What do you mean? I had to get you. You, uh..." My voice trails away as I look at Deacon over my shoulder. "You have to surprise Sabrina. You know, my cousin you were playing Santa for?"

"Of course...Sabrina." Jasper nods. He's probably running my action tape in his head and catching up on the lie.

Whether he's doing that or not, I don't know, but he follows along with the ruse. He sets his face in a bored, neutral expression, not giving Deacon any reason to question my lie.

He shrugs and grabs my hand, a smile forming on his face. "Come on, Holly. Let's go surprise your cousin and then get on with the night, shall we?"

Chapter 13

JASPER

"Good, this night has been one incident of needing a plan after another," Holly sighs, sitting in the sleigh and wrapping the blanket around her shoulders.

I still can't believe she came for me. Any other human would be back at home in bed, sleeping like a baby without another thought to my wellbeing. Most women I've met would have noped out the second I slid down their chimney. The fact that she got into the sleigh at all seems miraculous now that I have a moment to breathe.

She got in the sleigh. She helped me deliver presents. She took a taser hit and still let me kiss her. Then, she sucked my dick like no woman ever has.

Either she's borderline insane or she's the best woman in the world.

"New plan," I say, pushing the blow job out of my mind. I can try, anyway. I have half a chub just sitting by her.

"You actually have one? Did sitting in prison allow you time to ruminate?"

"In a word, yes. It's been enough time. The Tanners should be asleep. Hopefully, the sliding glass door we went out of is still unlocked."

"We're definitely going back?"

"We have to. I need the suit. You saw what happened when we tried this without a suit. Unless you want to punch a lot more punch cards tonight, I need to be able to get into houses and stay unseen. We're going to have to suck it up."

I park the sleigh back in the crop of evergreen trees. In front of us, the Tanner house is pitch black. Even the basement sliding door is dark. Either someone turned off the storage room bare bulb, or it burned out. If someone turned it off, they've been in the basement. I cross my fingers that the sliding door is still unlocked.

"I'm going to try the door. You stay here. Got it?"

"What if they're up and you get caught?"

"Take the sleigh home this time. Don't come for me."

She crinkles her lip in a sneer. "Fine."

"I know you're not happy about it. Just let me do this. I'm just going to try the sliding door, get in the sex room, and grab my suit and your tights. This is fine."

"Famous last words. Don't forget to give Darryl his chaps back."

I snap my fingers. "Chaps. Yes. I'll do that."

I kiss her on the forehead, take a deep breath, and jump out of the sleigh. This will work.

I hurdle the gate to the backyard and sprint to the sliding door. As soon as my fingers grab the handle, I don't feel give, and my heart deflates. They locked it. Looking back at the sleigh, Holly's covering her face with her hands.

I jump the fence again and plod to the sleigh. "Locked."

"Think they know we were there?"

I put my hands on my hips. "Probably not. If they were in the dungeon, my stuff is in the bin and behind a cabinet. Your tights weren't visible when we ran out of there. They're probably in bed."

"What do we do?" she asks, her voice quiet and practically a whisper.

This is the moment. I've been trained for this moment my whole life. It's the moment when a Santa comes face to face with a normal person. It's not something we actively invite, but it's something we plan for in case it happens. I'm a man. I'm not a boy that should slink around and shimmy up drainpipes or pick a lock. I'm going to man up.

"I'm going to ring the doorbell and ask for my suit back."

Holly shakes her head. "Nope. No way. What are you going to say? They won't believe it."

"I have to try. You stay here."

"I'm coming with you. But Jasper, how are you going to get them to believe you?"

I look around the sleigh like I expect a decoy present or reindeer to solve my problem. How am I going to get them to believe me? Sure, I can tell them about the time they got fuzzy handcuffs and nipple clamps a couple years ago or the time when Kristin was on the naughty list when she was eight. Would that be enough?

My eyes flick to the decoy presents again. "We'll take them a gift and explain what happened."

"What are we going to give them? All of the gifts in the back are spoken for and there's nothing in the decoy present boxes. Those are just for appearance."

"We still have their gifts," I say. I flex my jaw and square my shoulders back.

Holly rears back like I slapped her. Her eyes widen, and her hands cover her mouth and nose. I pull her hands down as she sticks her tongue out and looks like she's gagging. "Look at me, Holly."

"We can't…"

"We have to."

"I won't."

"I'll do it."

"We cannot take those toys back to them, Jasper. One of them has been inside your butt. The other has been in my…well, it's been in my vagina." She shakes her head. "I can't believe I just said that word to you."

"Why?" I ask, tilting my head. "It's the correct body part. I'm quite familiar with that particular part now. I'd classify it as a tasty snack."

She shakes her head and looks up at me again. "We just can't do it, Jasper."

"It'll be fine," I say, waving my hand like I'm swiping the entire problem aside. "Everyone washes sex toys when they get them out of the box anyway. We'll find a spare box in the warehouse, use the paper from a decoy present, and they won't know the difference."

"The smell may be a big indicator. I know if I got a new sex toy out and it smelled like it'd been in someone else's butt or any other hole, I probably wouldn't use it."

I shrug. I know the Tanners and know they wouldn't be bothered by it. They'd probably think it was a new marketing ploy for sex toys Like those stickers you can scratch and sniff. "They'll boil them and be right as rain, Holly. You have to trust me. I've seen what that couple has done since they met in high school. Used sex toys is the least of their concern. I'm much more concerned about them catching syphilis from their swinger partners." I put my hands on my hips and look around the sleigh. "If you have a better idea on how I can just walk up to their door at two in the morning and demand my pants back without at least offering them a present, I'd love to hear it."

"No, I do not." She closes her eyes and slowly shakes her head.

"Well, Dad always used to say that we go to war with the troops we have. This is what we have to work with, Holly."

She grabs the front of my bibs and pushes her forehead to my chest. "Just give me a minute to get my bearings. I won't let you go up to the door by yourself this time. It'll be less intimidating if there's a woman with you. Just let me...breathe for a moment."

I wrap my arms around her shoulders and hold her. I could hold her forever. It's cold and dregs of snow fly off the trees, landing in our hair. The moon shines overhead and even the owls are tired or just silent as they watch us decide if we're giving away used sex toys.

She's tired. I'm tired. Our bodies sag against each other in the cold air. I wish we were in a warm bed. Her bed. I wish my body was curled around her warmth as a fire crackled a few feet away. We'd wake after a long night's sleep and get in a warm bath together. I'd wash her hair, and she'd lay her head on my chest.

We have to get through tonight first.

She must think the same because she raises her head and widens her eyes, forcing them open. "Let's do this."

We work in silence as we carefully unwrap a decoy present to use the paper. Holly goes into the warehouse and finds tape while I put the used sex toys into the decoy present box. I'm tempted to give them a little rinse by running them through the snow, but that would cause more problems than it would solve. I'd be more suspicious of a sex toy with a dried-out pine needle or dirt stuck to the handle. When she comes back with the tape, the toys are already packed and ready for the paper to be folded neatly over it.

I let Holly take point on wrapping. Believe it or not, it's never been my specialty. The elves usually handle it, and I'm lucky to get the ends even when I fold over the paper. I'm a Santa that can't wrap a gift correctly.

When she's done, it's perfect, complete with gold and silver ribbon on top. We stare at it a few moments, both of us filled with regret that we're giving the Tanners used sex toys.

Blowing out a sigh that fluffs her bangs, Holly nods at me, spins toward the house, and I follow a few steps behind.

"Here goes nothing," she says, raising the knocker and letting it down before ringing the doorbell. "We need to give them a minute. They may be scared or deep sleepers. I know I always wonder if I imagined a noise when someone knocks or rings the bell in the middle of the night."

Holly waits a minute and rings the doorbell again, this time waiting a few seconds before knocking.

Thirty seconds later, there's a shuffling sound on the other side of the door. "Who is it?" a woman's voice asks.

"Hi, Kristin. It's Santa Claus."

Holly stares at me open-mouthed. "Really? You just hit her with it like a two-by-four in the face?"

"I thought honesty would be the best policy!"

"That sounds sus as fuck, Jasper. Would you just swing the door open and wave us in?"

There's silence on the other side of the wood. I put my hand on the door like I can calm Kristin by using magic. Putting my hand on the cold oak steadies me if nothing else. "Kristin, I came by to deliver your presents earlier tonight. But, well, I know about your sex room. I can prove I was there. Your storage room light was on, and your sliding door was unlocked when you came home tonight."

The door opens an inch, catching the chain. Smart woman. I only see half of her face, but her eyes are brown, and her hair is fire-engine red. I give a small wave and smile my best "I'm not a psycho here to kill you" smile.

Kristin looks out and runs her eyes up and down both of us, but she squints when she focuses on me. "What the hell are you wearing?"

"Who is it, Kristin?" Darryl asks from the other side of the door. He stomps toward us and joins his wife, half of his face appearing over hers. His beard is graying, and his silver hair is in a man bun.

"He says he's Santa."

"That's the screwiest Santa I've ever seen," Darryl chuckles. He doesn't shut the door in our faces, though. That's something.

"He knew the door was unlocked and the light was on," Kristin whispers to her husband.

I have to do something so they'll believe us. I never do this. I don't like bringing out the big guns, but Christmas for children depends on it. I look Darryl dead in the eyes and drop info like I'm dropping a deuce on his lap. "Darryl, when you were ten years old, you were interested in model trains. My father, the Santa at the time, got you one. But your father didn't want you interested in anything but tools. Who knows why he didn't like the model trains, but he burned the train set in the backyard. I know you wrote for the next two years, asking for a new set. We never delivered because we knew it would end up in the burn pit. My father put you on the list to get whatever you want for the rest of your life as long as you ask. You still write us every year, and we deliver every single time."

"Is that true? Did your dick dad do that?" Kristin asks Darryl.

Darryl stares at me, and I hold his gaze. "I never told anyone that."

I take a deep breath. "You know I exist because you still write me, and you get the yearly gifts." Darryl and Kristin both nod. "I don't have my suit because I also know about your sex room. If you go down to your basement, you'll find this lovely lady's tights." I gesture to Holly, and she waves. "You'll find the top of my suit behind one of the cabinets on the far wall. My pants are in your BDSM bin. If you go check, I'd appreciate it. You don't need to unlock the door. We'll wait here." I take a step back and pull Holly with me, trying to show Darryl and Kristin that we're not here simply to get entrance into their house. "We just want our clothes back...and to apologize for violating your privacy like that."

"Why did you go down there?" Darryl asks.

"See the woman next to me?" I gesture at Holly. "I had a chance to have fun with her in your sex room, and I took it. I know you, Darryl. You may not know me, but I know a lot about you. I know that you understand that feeling. The feeling of wanting to be with a woman so badly, that you make poor decisions."

Darryl looks at Kristin and chews his lip, thinking. He looks back at Holly, who looks at the ground. I hope I didn't royally embarrass her, but I thought the truth was necessary here.

"Close the door and lock it while I go check," he instructs Kristin.

I nearly fall on the floor in relief as Kristin locks the door in our faces. It's fine. Darryl will go downstairs, find our clothes, and we'll exchange them for their Christmas gift. I slide my hand into Holly's and squeeze it. "I'm sorry if that made you feel awkward. I had to tell them what we did."

She gives a wry smile. "Well, you didn't tell them all of it. I mean, they don't know the details."

She leans her head on my shoulder and closes her eyes until loud footsteps sound on the other side of the door. When the door opens, it opens all the way, revealing Darryl's barrel chest and white tank top all rural men must own. His boxer shorts have ducks on them, but I don't care what he's wearing. It's all I can do not to hug the man since he's holding Holly's tights in one hand and my suit in the other.

"I don't suppose you'll tell me why you need these so bad. Just seems like regular clothes," he says, running his eyes up and down my suit.

"Would you believe me if I said that's the only thing that gets me into a house unseen? That's why we knocked. I have to have them back."

Darryl hands them over and smiles. "Well, I can't be responsible for Santa Claus not being able to deliver presents to children. I'd have a place in hell for sure."

I take the suit and flex my hands against the cotton. If it wouldn't be indecent, I'd drop the bibs right here and jump into it. But Kristin's looking over Darryl's shoulder, still scared.

"I almost forgot! Here are your presents for the year," I say, holding the package out to them. "There's something in there for both of you." I feel Holly stiffen beside me, probably trying to keep from gagging. "Uh...Merry Christmas."

Darryl smiles like a child, showing a gap between his teeth. "Well, Merry Christmas to you!"

"Sorry about the middle of the night wake up, and I'll see you next year. Feel free to go big on present requests."

"I'll do that. You take care."

He shuts the door on us, and we wait until the living room light flicks off before looking at each other slowly. I hand over her tights, and she grabs them like they'll burn my hand if I hold them any longer.

I pull her to me for a hug and smile against her skin. "Let's get the fuck out of here before they sniff their gifts."

Chapter 14

HOLLY

"Who's next?" I ask, clapping my hands and rolling my shoulders.

I'm pumped. Amped. Ready to take on the world. I could run a marathon or punch through a wall. My second wind hit me around the time Jasper pulled up his pants, put on his suit jacket, and flexed his fingers like he was absorbing an ancient magical power that turns him into the world's best cat burglar.

Which is kind of what he is, except he puts stuff *in* a house instead of taking it out.

"Blaze Morgenstern. Age eight. Small red box," Jasper says, switching from navigation to a spreadsheet on his tablet.

"Got it. Is this a video game?" I ask, holding the present to my ear and shaking it.

"Most of them are. Spoiler alert. I look forward to getting letters *not* asking for some kind of video game. I think they're quaint."

I pass him the present from my spot standing on the ladder at the back of the sleigh, and he disappears down the Morganstern chimney, only to appear a few seconds later.

"Next up, Lane Morris."

I duck down to the bin below me that contains presents for the children of South Dakota, which is our current location, and I don't even hold on for dear life when the sleigh takes off again. I'm getting used to the jostle of takeoff and landing. Add that to things I never thought I'd be able to say.

I rustle through the bin until I find Lane Morris's gift – a large package that rattles when I shake it. It's heavy and definitely not a video game.

"Here you go," I say, popping up into the night air again. I'm not even getting sick when I look down. Funny how a time crunch and adrenaline rush can do that. "What is this one?"

Jasper closes his eyes and smiles. "Chemistry set. This girl likes science and has a propensity toward blowing things up. Let's just hope nobody gets hurt this year."

"Huh. I think I rather like this little girl," I say, handing him the gift.

Jasper takes the package, lands on a two-story apartment building, and jumps out to go through an upstairs window. He's back out of the building before I can blink. "How are you doing that so fast?" I ask.

"Once I'm in, I just drop it on the floor under the tree and get the fuck out. I'm not filling anyone's stockings tonight. No time."

"Fair enough."

"Oh, I brought you cookies." Jasper unfolds a paper napkin with poinsettias on it to reveal two chocolate chip cookies and three sugar cookies that were clearly made by a child, judging by the spotty icing and clumped sprinkles. "Best perk of the job."

"Did you bring me milk?"

"Do you want me to steal the glass?" he asks with a smile. "I can't have you bailing me out again for something little. South Dakota police don't have punch cards to the parlor. We can't risk it, especially since Lane Morris's father is the mayor around here and her mother is a police officer. I'm not risking stealing their dishes."

I take a bite of one of the chocolate chip cookies and suck on the chocolate that's still slightly warm. These are no store-bought cookies. I nearly swoon. I shouldn't be this excited about a cookie, but it's all I've had to eat for hours except a few licks of a candy cane.

"Let's get this done so I can take you for a proper breakfast," Jasper says, taking the reins and making the takeoff noise he uses to spur on the reindeer. "Next up in the bag is Leti Lee Lightfoot. Another video game."

"Bacon or sausage?" Jasper asks, holding out a stack of sandwiches on top of a drink carrier containing coffee in paper cups. One sandwich is marked as sausage. The other two are marked with a bacon sticker.

I've never been so tired, not even after the bus full of ministers on the way to the revival. Even thinking about going to work in a few hours is surreal as I watch the sun rise over the shower station for truckers next door. It's hard to believe what's happened in the last several hours when I'm sitting on the curb outside a gas station outside of who knows where.

Jasper and I are both exhausted. If his face mirrors mine, I must be a clusterfuck wreck. His hair sticks out in every direction, and his beard stubble isn't stubble any longer as it gets close to a full-on beard. His eyes are droopy with dark circles under them, and his suit hangs loosely off his shoulder like he just did a triathlon in it. In a way, we did.

He still looks yummy enough to eat, even after working our asses off for the past few hours. Well, it's been hours for the world. To us, even with manipulating time a bit, it's felt like an entire day.

We did everything we were supposed to do. We hit every house. Sure, we did it half-assed. Jasper threw the presents where he thought they had the best chance of being found, ignored the stockings, and left the cookies and milk alone at most houses.

But we got it done. Every last kid has a present. Something akin to pride fills my chest that I helped every nice kid in the world who was good and wrote to Santa. Somewhere a kid is opening their gift right now and excited because Jasper was there.

"Always bacon," I say, grabbing the wrapped breakfast sandwich. I deserve bacon, preferably the type that's crispy and almost burnt.

Jasper shoves a small bag in his pocket and sits down next to me on the curb, briefly glancing at the lot across the street where the sleigh is parked behind the in-progress construction site for a dentist's office. If people think it's odd to see a man dressed as Santa outside a gas station at five in the morning, they don't comment on it as they walk around us. They've probably seen weirder shit at a gas station this time of day, even on Christmas. I've certainly seen weirder shit tonight.

"I'm so hungry, I could eat a gas station breakfast sandwich." I unwrap the sandwich and bite into it. The buttermilk biscuit flakes in my hands, and I throw my head back in pleasure as soon as the salty bacon hits my tongue. "Good," I mumble around the mouthful of biscuit, bacon, egg, and cheese.

"I knew from the moment I met you that I wanted to buy you breakfast," Jasper says, opening his coffee lid flap and blowing on the steam. "I didn't think it would be quite like this, though."

I swallow and take a sip of my own coffee. It's still too hot, so I place it next to me and focus on filling my stomach. "What exactly did you imagine?"

He turns to me as he unwraps the sausage biscuit. "When I met you yesterday, I imagined taking you to breakfast."

"Yesterday feels a million years away."

"That's the damn truth." Jasper takes a bit of food, chews, and swallows before taking a sip of his scalding coffee. "When I saw you in the waiting room, that's what came into my mind – waking up next to you in a soft bed with crisp white sheets, rolling over, and asking you to breakfast at some nice brunch place."

"Like the type that serves eggs over easy and adds spice to their bacon?" I ask.

"Yes. With thick French toast with strawberries and whipped cream. Oh, and don't forget mimosas. When I imagine it, you're wearing one of my t-shirts."

I groan a little at the idea of a nice breakfast with him. Will I see him again after he drops me off? Will I ever get to wear his t-shirt and pull the fabric up to my face so I can smell him?

We eat and drink our coffee in silence and watch the movement around us. People in cars packed with presents wash their windshields, pump gas, and walk in and out of the station. Jasper eats his sausage sandwich, and we split the other bacon sandwich. Jasper tears it in half and hands it to me without asking. I take it and savor it as cars pull in and out of the parking spots around us.

I sniff and look around at the trees in the area and the birds just starting to peek out of their nests for the morning. "Where are we?" I ask.

"Michigan and Ohio border."

"Not too far from home, huh?"

"I should have you home in less than an hour or so." He looks down at his boots and wiggles his toes. "What time do you have to work?"

He sounds sad. Is he thinking of me giving another man or multiple men hand jobs today? My stomach roils at the thought. I've never been squeamish about my job, but the idea of touching a man other than him repulses me now. It's just friction on a dick and doesn't mean anything, but it meant something with him.

It all meant *a lot* with him.

"Noon. But Mom's going to need her meds in a couple hours. If she wakes up and I'm not there, she may be scared. Helena will be rolling out to work, and she'll get worried if I'm not home soon, especially if she realizes I didn't come home last night."

Jasper's quiet a moment and rubs the back of his neck. "Holly?"

"Yeah?"

"Tonight meant a lot to me. Nobody has ever done so much to help me. When you figured out everything and then came to get me from the station, that was just..."

His voice trails off, and I press my index finger to his mouth, smiling. "Shush. I loved helping you."

If it wouldn't be weird since we just met yesterday, I'd offer to be his ride-or-die girl for as long as he'd have me.

He looks to the construction site and pushes himself up from the curb, crumbling his last sandwich wrapper in his fist. "I feel like we've known each other forever, like you're a friend I went to school with or something. Thanks for coming with me. It couldn't have been easy to get on my sleigh."

He offers his hand, and I take it. I teeter a little when I stand, and Jasper wraps his arms around me. Once I'm stable, he doesn't let go. We stand there and hug on the Michigan and Ohio border while the sun comes up, neither one of us wanting to let go. It may be because he wants to hug me. It may also be that we're the only thing holding each other up.

Chapter 15

JASPER

Holly opens her eyes when the sleigh lands with a thump on her roof. She slept for the last twenty minutes, and I didn't have the heart to wake her. She looked so peaceful with her eyes closed and a slow line of drool dripping out of the corner of her mouth. I wiped it away a couple of times for her, but at least she doesn't snore.

"Are we home?" Holly asks in a weak voice. I hate that she moves away from me. Even though she was drooling, I liked her leaning against my shoulder.

"Last stop. Want me to carry you downstairs?"

She rubs sleep out of her eyes and blinks twice. "Do I need you to carry me? No. Would I want you to carry me just so I could be close to you another minute?"

"I'll do it." I move her hair back from her face and place a kiss on her forehead. It's one of those slow kisses where I let my lips linger, absorbing the heat of her skin.

I should say something. I should ask to see her again or ask her to a movie next week. I should offer to come another day and take her to a better breakfast than gas station sandwiches. That would be the proper thing to do.

Would she even want me long-term? I live in Canada and have a weird job. She also has a weird job, but she isn't known the world over for it with lots of work stress one night of the year, to say nothing of a legion of elves and a team of reindeer to command. I can't imagine how hard it would be for a woman to wrap her head around my life and the responsibility day in and day out. She probably thinks I'm a fun time for a night, and she's kind enough to make sure presents get delivered to the children of the world.

But something long-term? I'm destined to have my heart ripped from my chest and shown to me before she walks away.

Holly pulls back the blanket that was over her lap and moves to get out of the sleigh. Think, dummy! Do something to impress her before she gets out and walks into her house.

"I almost forgot," I say, pulling the bag out of my pants. "I got you something from the gas station."

Holly smiles a fake smile, bats her eyes, and places her hands flat under her chin. "Just what a lady dreams of hearing."

I laugh and open the bag to root around for one of the items I purchased. Finding it, I grip it in my hand and pull it out of the bag without showing it to Holly. "Close your eyes."

"Jasper, you shouldn't have."

"Open your hand," I direct.

She does as I ask, and I marvel at how trusting she is of me. I can't help but drag my finger over the palm of her hand, sending up a silent prayer to whatever entity is listening that it's not the last time I touch her hands. I place the item in her hand and close her fingers over it. "OK, you can open your eyes."

She opens her eyes and her hand at the same time. When she opens them, laughter rumbles from her chest, and her smile widens so I can see her back teeth. She clutches the item to her chest and places a kiss on my cheek. "You shouldn't have."

"Geez, Holly, it's just a magnet that says, 'I put the big O in Ohio.'"

"I love it."

"I didn't give you the big O in Ohio, though. I made you come in Pennsylvania. I don't think they make magnets saying something like 'I gave you the P in Pennsylvania.'"

She waves her hand. "Eh, it's a border state. Close enough. That's a hell of a slogan, by the way. Our state travel bureau should look into it."

"We can go back to Ohio real quick if you're interested in the big O – "

She shoves me, and I catch her hand, squeezing it in the process. "Good night, Holly Hepperdine. Well, I guess it's morning. Have a good day, Holly Hepperdine."

"What else was in the bag?" she asks, already reaching for the bag with the hand I'm not holding. "I saw something else in there."

I pull away. "Just something for the sleigh in case we needed it. You have to get back."

We wrestle a little until she pulls the small plastic bag from my pocket. I reach for it, and she slaps my hand away. "What are you hiding?"

"Uh, nothing."

She opens the bag and rolls her eyes. "Condoms? Hopeful, huh?"

"It was just a precaution in case you couldn't control yourself around my dick, but we don't have time."

"Who says?"

"You have to give your mom her meds." I gesture to the house below us.

Holly looks at the snow falling in the early morning light. There's a quiet about her. It's also quiet around us since it's too early for anyone to be out and about on Christmas morning. It's cloudy and dark for this time of day, the snow picking up and hitting us in the face when the wind blows. "I have thirty minutes before Mom needs her meds. There's always time for Christmas magic."

My head jolts up. "Yeah?"

Pulling me to her, she buries her face in my chest, inhaling deeply. "Yeah. I can't leave without saying goodbye, you know? I can't think of a better way to top off the night."

My hands wind in her hair, and I tilt her head back until she's looking at me with those maddening eyes. If I never see her again – and who could blame her if she's done with me after tonight – I'll never get them out of my head or stop dreaming about them.

I kiss the tip of her nose and grin against her skin. "I want to say goodbye to you properly. Think those tights can come off for me one more time?"

She reaches down and pulls her tights down her legs in one movement, bringing the panties with her and kicking everything to the side. She pauses and picks up her panties before pulling them out of her tights and handing them to me. "Here. A souvenir."

"I get to keep them?"

"You got me a magnet. I'll give you my panties. You seem to like them, so it's a fair trade."

I shove them in my pants pocket again and grab her hips until she's straddling me. She goes limp in my arms like she trusts me and anything I want to do to her, and her lips meet mine in a lazy kiss.

Looking up at her, I take a mental snapshot of just how beautiful she is on my lap. The snow in her hair. Her hair framing her face. My hands move up her hips until the skirt is back up around her waist where it belongs when she's on my lap.

She undoes my pants before I know what's happening, and she takes a condom out of the small package, tears it open, and rolls it down my erect length. I buck into her hand as she rolls the condom on. Every nerve in my body sings, and my eyes flutter shut when her fingers trace the head of my dick as she pinches the end of the rubber.

She runs her hands through my hair before bringing her finger to my chin, tilting it to look up at her. "Look at me, Jasper. I want to see you."

I open my eyes. As hard as it is, I need to look at her as she slides down my shaft. I force my eyes open, even as hers close when she impales herself to the hilt with a groan. I moan in return like we've lost the ability to talk and can only communicate in grunts and gurgling noises.

She wraps her arms around my back and pushes her face into my neck. "Fuck, Jasper. You feel just like I thought you would. Deep. Hard."

I grip her hips and pull her into me as I thrust up, not able to get enough of her. Her pussy tightens around me with every inhale of her breath and relaxes when she exhales. I can time when her pussy will tighten and release once I get the rhythm of her breath against my jaw. I throw my head back against the headrest, and she drops warm kisses across my neck while she rides me.

When I do look down, I catch the reindeer watching me fuck Holly. Their blinking eyes watch us without a sound, and they don't move. Honestly, I couldn't give a shit right now if I have an audience of animals that are supposed to respect me as the new Santa soon. I'm too busy consuming this woman.

I take deep breaths to inhale her scent, committing it to memory. I need to remember the smell of her skin. I inhale the slight scent and taste of the bacon sandwich on her lips, and the smell of her hair with the slight hint of apple shampoo as loose strands trail my upper lip. The earthy scent of her not-recently-showered body isn't offensive. It's arousing and natural. Something in the human evolutionary line must make us love the smell of a woman's sweat and want. A drop of sweat runs down her temple, and I lick it away, savoring the salty taste on my tongue.

Our mouths meet as she grinds down hard on my cock. "Jasper," she hisses when I move my finger around to her asshole.

"Do you like that when you're fucked?"

"Yes," she moans. "Just a little. Not a lot. And don't pull it out like you're starting a lawn mower."

I chuckle and flick the tip of my finger over her puckered hole. The sensation pushes her into me further, and she brings her hand to her clit. "Yeah," I coo, nipping at her neck. "Help me out. I bet you like everything rubbed down there all at once, don't you?"

I heckle her, nudging her with my nose. I teasingly kiss her collarbone and pull my finger away from her asshole until she whines for it back. Only when she stops rubbing her clit, do I resume playing with her butt. We push and pull at each other until her entire body tightens.

Desperate, I use my free hand to pull her shirt up and move her bra away from a nipple. The cold air has the pale pink nub pointed and practically trembling for my mouth. She rubs her clit harder and faster as soon as I latch onto it, sucking and licking. Fuck, even her tits taste good. Does every part of her taste good?

"I'm going to come, Jasper. Don't stop! Please don't stop."

I come off her nipple to groan in pleasure at the sound of her voice while she's about to come on my dick. She sounds so urgent – so pleased with what I'm doing to her.

She clenches around me and arches her back as my teeth clamp gently over her upper breast. I don't draw blood or bite hard enough to bruise. It's just a love bite to let her know that she may be enjoying an electrifying orgasm, but I'm still down here. Still here for her and wanting her to come but also wanting her grounded with me. We're in this together like we've been together in some form of shit all night.

I lap at the small red mark I made, and pride swells through my chest. It may be vampiric and filthy, but she's mine now, even if the mark will be gone in an hour. Her eyes flutter, oblivious to any pain or enjoying the combination of pain and her orgasm coiling through her body. If I had to guess, it's the latter. She moans and whimpers my name as she grips her legs tighter on my sides. She bucks, arches, and squirms over me until she shatters around my cock, shaking and trembling.

The world tilts on its axis, and stars burst behind my eyelids as her pussy throbs around me. I can't get close enough to her. I want to consume her or crawl into her chest and stay there. The idea of pulling my cock from her body and separating is unthinkable. I'm damned to miss this woman for all eternity if I can't figure out a way to be with her.

My mind splits into several thoughts. Love. Adoration. The obsession to figure out a way to be with her, even if it means giving up everything I've ever known and everything I've been destined to become. I'll give it up in a heartbeat if she asks, but I know she never would. I may die of the pleasure she gives me. I may die from a gorgeous woman riding my dick in my father's sleigh.

I will destroy anyone or anything that comes between my quest to be with her. I need to take this sleigh home, do the after-Christmas duties we usually do, check on Dad, and get the fuck back to bumfuck Pennsylvania to get this woman.

I hope she misses me while I get back home to handle business. Maybe giving her a couple of days to center and think about our options is what we need.

With a grunt, I release into the condom as she swirls her hips and coos filth into my ear that I don't process because I'm not thinking straight. I can't think of anything but *more*. I want more. I have to have more.

We stay entwined and sweaty for minutes until she kisses me on the cheek and slides off my lap. I force my limbs to work and unroll the full condom, wrapping it in the plastic bag from the gas station. I'll dump it in the trash when I get home.

She quietly rolls on her tights yet again, and I buckle my pants. When I look up, the reindeer are still staring. "What are you looking at?" I grunt at Prancer. She's not the only one looking, but she's the only one I can practically see smirking. If reindeer can be Olympic judges for the sex event, she stares at me like she's the Korean judge and giving me a six for the dismount. "I know you've never seen a Santa get laid before, but I feel you judging."

"Is this the part where I say thanks?" Holly asks. Her voice is quiet and husky like she slept all night instead of delivering toys with me.

"Thanks for the sex?" I ask, chuckling. "That's so cliché in movies, huh?"

She bites her lips and wipes sweat from her collarbone. "Thanks for the night, Jasper. It was definitely an adventure. I can honestly say I've never had a night like that."

"It was an adventure to meet you."

She looks at the sky like she's trying to find the sun behind the thick clouds to tell time. "I hate saying goodbye, but I really have to get Mom's medicine in her."

I grab her hand and turn it over to place a kiss on the palm. I don't know why I do it. Maybe it's because I think this is the only part of her body that I haven't kissed tonight. "Merry Christmas."

Chapter 16

HOLLY

I don't know what I expected. At the end of the day, I'm just a sex worker. He's the next Santa, for fuck's sake. Did I think he was going to Richard Gere me and show up with a limo to climb a fire escape with a rose in his teeth?

"Holly! Client for you," Linda One yells at the top of her voice. I sigh and drop the cleaning rag into the laundry bin. We really need to get an intercom system or something.

I round the corner with hope in my chest that it's Jasper, only to be disappointed when I see an older man with salt and pepper hair and worn brown work pants at the front desk. The man smiles, and one of his canines is missing.

Fuck my life.

It was bad that I'd jerk off these guys before, but I can't stand it now. It's not them or the fact that the job can get messy. It's me.

It's *Jasper*. It's fucking Jasper that walked into my life and made me feel, for one entire night, that I could really get away from my life. That I could be something special or do something I was meant to do.

None of these guys are him. None of the men I've scrolled through on Tinder in the last week are Jasper. Will it be like this forever? Will I always search my waiting room for him when Linda One calls me to meet a client, hoping Santa's son has come back for another hand job?

Where the fuck is he?

We had something. I know we did. I felt it, and it wasn't just sexual. Our banter was fire. There were feelings between us we didn't put into words. I know I didn't make any of it up in my head, even though I woke up on Christmas morning after he dropped me off and thought it was all a dream.

Was it?

Was this a bad *Dallas* season finale with everything being a nog-induced sex dream brought on by my jerk-off session with Jasper and watching too much Dean Winchester?

I went up to my roof on the day after Christmas. When Mom asked what I was doing with the old wooden ladder from the garage, I told her I suspected squirrels in the attic again and needed to look near the chimney to see if there was an entrance. I was searching the chimney alright, but I was looking for hoof prints. I searched for sleigh drag marks across the roof. I sifted through the snow for left behind glitter or tinsel. I wanted something to prove that Jasper and a legion of flying reindeer were real and on the roof the night before.

Too bad it snowed again before I could get up there.

But there was one thing I couldn't explain – a small red mark just above my left breast that lasted a few hours. I can't bite myself there, and none of my clients have been near that spot. No rabid dog has come into my room, and I haven't been near any serial biters. Only one thing could have left that mark, and I held onto that red spot all of Christmas. I even took a picture of it before it faded because it confirms that I haven't lost my marbles.

I found the magnet under my pillow yesterday. I must have stuck it there before I took a two-hour nap after Jasper dropped me off. He's real. There's no way I would have driven to the Michigan and Ohio border on Christmas to buy a gas station magnet. I shoved it in my purse to look at it when I'm at work or running errands. I'll always keep it with me.

Somehow, a gas station magnet is the most valuable thing I own.

"Holly," Linda One says, snapping her manicured nails in front of my face. "This is a client." She gestures to the man like he's an honored guest. "Speak to him."

"Sorry," I say, shaking my head like I can shake off thoughts of Jasper. Fat fucking chance. "Are you ready to go back? Full service?"

"Yep. Full release," the man drawls. He knows the drill if he's asking for full release. This isn't his first rodeo, and he licks his lips at my breasts, inspecting them closer like he needs glasses.

"Come on back, sir," I deadpan.

I turn and stiffly wave over my shoulder for the man to follow me. My voice has zero enthusiasm in it, and I haven't been able to appear excited about my job. My tips have gone down this week, and I go home every night and cry. Not because my job is awful. I cry because I want Jasper to come back. I cry for the accounting degree I don't use. I cry because I've applied to jobs every day this week, and the rejections are starting to roll in.

I cry because the police are starting to come in with their punch cards, and it's getting hard to explain to Linda One why almost every cop in the county has a full punch card.

Something has to break before I do.

Once in my massage room, I wave toward the table like I couldn't care less if the man gets on it. "Go ahead and get comfortable. Take your pants off."

The man looks at the table and climbs on. "Linda Two always warms her hands and tells me a joke." He kicks his shoes off.

"Do I look like a comedian? Is this an improv show?" I ask. The man cringes and averts his eyes to the ceiling. "Isn't it enough that I'm going to yank on your dick? Do you want me to tap dance while I'm at it? Maybe saw a coworker in half? Am I a fucking magician too?"

"No, sorry. I, uh, just thought it was fun. It relaxes me."

I blow out a sigh as the man closes his eyes, probably not wanting to look at the surly bitch putting on rubber gloves. I shouldn't be mean to him. He doesn't have a wife, as evidenced by the lack of a wedding ring. Unless he has a girlfriend, he's not a cheater like some guys that come in here. Something tells me that's not an option with him. This is literally his release, something to fill his needs so he can function in society without going on a rampage due to lack of sex. He pays cold, hard cash. Mom's meds are low, and the prescription price just went up. I certainly need cold, hard cash.

I put my hands on the table and don't even wipe my face as tears eke out my eyes. "I'm sorry, sir. I didn't mean to bitch at you. I'm usually a friendly tugger, but it's been a bad week."

The man covers his dick and looks at the ceiling. "Um, are we going to talk about it?"

"I won't burden you with my bullshit. That's not why you're here."

"I'm a bartender. I'm used to it. Spill." He may be looking at my tits, but his voice is kind.

Now I really feel like an asshole. I may have judged him for his worn pants and his missing tooth, but he could be a nice guy. A drunk patron could have knocked the tooth out, and he may be as broke as my family, not able to afford a thousand-dollar dental implant. A hundred-dollar hand job, funded by half a night's tips, may be all he can afford to brighten his life.

"It's mental, and you'll run screaming from the room."

"I've heard some shit in my day. Try to dazzle me with something new, sweetheart."

"I was swept away by Santa Claus's son last week. He took me on a sleigh ride to help with inventory after I gave him a great hand job. We got caught a couple times, he was arrested wearing assless chaps, and I had to punch the punch cards of most of the police force to get him out of jail. We had the best sex of my life in the sleigh while the reindeer watched, and we played with someone else's anal bead wand and dildo before boxing them up as new. He dropped me off after the delivery, and I haven't heard from him since."

Silence fills the room until the man bites his lip. His eyes widen. "I've never heard shit like that, young lady. Are you OK? Are you willing to talk to a professional?"

I turn away from him and reach for the lube on the cabinet. "I'm fine. Drop your pants. Let's get this party started."

He undoes his pants and pulls them down so I can see he's at full mast. His short, veiny dick bobs in his huge nest of pubic hair, and I heave out a sigh. Can you miss a guy's manscaped area? Is that a thing? Tears form in my eyes but not for the ugly dick in front of me. Tears form because I miss Jasper's body. All of it.

As I reach for the man's cock to grip the base, a scuffle comes from the hallway. Beyond the doorway, Linda One yells something inaudible. The man on the table leans up onto his elbows and turns his ear toward the door.

I freeze. Is someone hurting Linda One? Is there a disgruntled client? I move to lock the door as a heavy weight sinks into my stomach.

"I just want to talk to her," a voice says, coming closer.

I know that voice!

"Jasper?" I yell, dropping the bottle of lube in my hand so that it falls on the table and squirts everywhere. I'll clean it up later.

I'm halfway to the door when it bursts open, and Jasper enters the room in dark jeans, a black sweater with the sleeves pushed up past his forearms, and some kind of waterproof boots with laces untied at the top. He looks positively yummy. Relaxed. Handsome.

Mine. I want him to be mine.

He startles at the sight of the man on the table, my rubber gloves, and the man wiping a glob of lube off his forehead. Jasper squints and reddens. "Uh...sorry, bro. I just need to talk to Holly for a few moments."

Jasper reaches for my hand and then pulls his hand back, looking at my gloves and cringing. He looks at his own hands like he's unsure if he touched me yet.

"Oh, I haven't started yet. Clean gloves." I wave my hands in the air like I'm making jazz hands.

"Good. I'm in time."

"Um, am I going to be jerked off?" the man on the table asks. "I paid money for this."

"I'll be with you in a moment, sir," I say as Linda One comes into the room, gasps, and closes the door. She probably doesn't want the outburst to disturb other clients or doesn't want someone walking by to see the man's dick as he relaxes prone on the table like none of this is awkward.

"What are you doing here, Jasper?" I ask, letting him take my hands.

He kisses me on my forehead in such a loving way, I practically swoon into him. "I would have been here sooner, but there are things I have to do after a delivery run. Inventory. After parties. Bonuses for the staff. Dad got worse, and he's in hospice now. It's been nuts."

"I'm so sorry, Jasper. Is he still alive?"

"Yes, but he's not doing well. It won't be long." He glances at the man on the table as the man's hand wanders to his own dick. Jasper points. "Is he going to jerk himself off while I'm in here?"

"Sir, are you getting started without me?"

"I'm on a time crunch. My break is over at five." The man grabs another glob of spilled lube from the table and starts rubbing his own length, complete with a thwacking sound as his hand moves back and forth over his dick.

Jasper shrugs and looks back at me. "This is really unromantic and not at all how I pictured this, but I'm here for you, Holly! I had to come get you. I thought I could drop you off and move along my merry way, but I realize I can't. I can't live another day knowing that you're in the world and I'm not sitting next to you."

"Why me? I don't understand," I say, gesturing to the man still jerking off on my table. The man's mouth is open in pleasure like he's oblivious to the conversation. "You could have a million women. You're handsome, and you're fucking Santa Claus." I glance at the man on the table, but if he registered the Santa remark, he doesn't comment. "Look what I do for a living."

"You shouldn't sell yourself short like that," the man on the table says. Obviously, he is paying attention. Maybe he thinks Jasper is a mall Santa. "Your profession is one of the oldest, and you're still a human being. You provide a service and contribute to the local economy as a consumer and a taxpayer."

"Thank you," I say, patting his shoulder.

"Your profession doesn't matter to me, but you don't need to do this any longer, sweetheart," Jasper says. He runs his hand through my hair, and I lean into his palm. It's strong and warm. Like home.

"I don't have an accounting job, Jasper. I need to buy Mom's meds and take care of her. Look around this town! It's devoid of any job opportunities. Helena can't pay for tuition and her other expenses alone. I need this job until I can find something remote or even get a business loan to start my own LLC."

The man on the table gestures for me to come closer, and I move next to him as he grabs my boob through my tank top with his free hand. I ignore it and so does Jasper. He moves with me, coming to the table and standing in front of me, ignoring the man jerking off inches away and the man accidentally rubbing Jasper's chest while he's palming my breasts.

Jasper pushes his forehead to mine. It may be a cliché, but he smells like peppermint. Toothpaste, perhaps. "Come work for me."

I raise my head. "What?"

"The last few days have taught me one thing. OK, two things. Number one, I like you. I haven't enjoyed someone's company like that in years. I want to see where this goes between us. I don't care that you had a job where you gave hand jobs. As long as I'm the guy you give hand jobs to in the future, I don't care about the past. Number two, I need help with bookkeeping and inventory. You're fucking brilliant, Holly. The way you handled everything on Christmas Eve and the way you can think on your feet when something goes wrong...well, I can't find elves for that. Come work for me and be my operations manager."

"This sounds like a really good opportunity for you. You should take it," the man on the table pants. He rubs his balls and squirms, clenching his butt cheeks and arching off the table.

"Let's go in the hallway," I whisper to Jasper. "We'll let this gentleman finish his business."

"Where am I supposed to...put it?" the man on the table asks. "Do you have a tissue, or should I take off my sock?"

Jasper quickly hands the man a wad of tissues from my table before grabbing my hand and pulling me out to the hallway. I realize I still have my gloves on, so I take them off and throw them on the carpet without a care for the fact that I'll either have to pick them up later or explain why I'm littering in the hallway to Linda One. Jasper grabs my hands again, and I squeeze back, relishing the warmth of his fingers without the gloves.

"What about my mom? I can't leave her."

"I've thought of that. Bring her. We have plenty of room. I'll even go with you to explain the whole thing to her. She'll get the best medical care, and Canadian prescription costs are lower than American costs, even if you're not a citizen. We'll take care of her, Holly, and we'll do it together. As a team. We already know we work well together. You and I together? The world wouldn't be able to stop us. You fill the gaps of my weaknesses. I will help you with whatever you need."

A loud groan comes from my massage room, and Jasper and I stare at each other without blinking as the man probably unloads into the wad of tissue. We stare at each other as I think about the offer, biting my lip.

Could I move in with Jasper? Helena's old enough to stay in our house and go to school. Maybe she can have a couple of roommates move in and pay rent to make up the cost of the mortgage and taxes. I could work with Jasper. That way, if it doesn't work out, I can always come back to the house and start again.

I could *try* with Jasper.

This kind of offer doesn't come along every day, and my stomach roils with nerves. Moving. Living with a man for the first time in my life. Explaining to my mother that Santa is real and regularly uses anal bead wands with her daughter. I liked those and want that to be a regular thing. My thighs clench together at the thought.

"There's a lot to consider," I tell Jasper. "I want to try. I want to see if this works between us. It's just scary. Would operations mean I have to boss around elves? If it doesn't work out with us, how can I put that on a job application as past employment? Not to mention there's a lot to moving. I mean...Canada is a scary place."

He crinkles his forehead and cocks his head to the side. Before he can respond, the man comes out of the room and zips his pants. He nods to me, and I stop him before he gets to the end of the hall. "Sir, tell Linda One to refund your money."

The man turns around, "Will you get in trouble? It sounds like you're having a rough time, and I don't want you to get fired, sweetheart. We all have rough days."

"She won't fire me," I say, smiling and looking back at Jasper. His eyes plead with me to make a choice, and there's no way I can say no to those eyes. "I just quit."

One Year Later...

HOLLY

"**I**t has to be sturdy," I say, flipping over the toy in my hand and checking the back. A small crack runs down the center. "Replace this. We only give perfect, well-made toys. Get it on the sleigh before three New York time."

The elf I'm addressing hurries off, and I shake my head. It still throws me off that elves aren't short. That elf was at least six inches taller than me.

I toss the broken toy on my desk and look at my workspace. Only Jasper's office is bigger. Snow falls outside my window, and Christmas lights line the crown molding along the ceiling. My desk is bigger than my first car, and a jar of stereotypical candy canes is available for any elves who want to stop by and have one. The previous operations managers were obviously male, as evidenced by the dark panel walls, but I've made the place more feminine with photos of Jasper, Helena, and my mother.

My mother adjusted well here. I take care of her or read to her for about an hour a day, but Jasper has hired care for her while I work. They handle the hard parts of caregiving. I can't lift her for bathing, and I'm thankful for the hired staff. Some of the older, retired elves have befriended her, and she's not quite so pale now, even if the sun rarely shines this far north. Her cheeks are rosy, and she talks excitedly of her new friends and caregivers like that may have been what she was missing all along.

It was hard telling Mom that Santa was real and we were moving to Canada to help Santa run the workshop. Like any normal human, she didn't believe it at first. She only believed it when Jasper visited, showed her how the suit worked, and then showed her the reindeer and sleigh. Like mother, like daughter.

I love him, though. I worried that I'd get to Canada and we'd fall apart. That didn't happen. In fact, working as a team for the last year has been everything any human being could hope for. Jasper supports me through everything, and I've done everything in my power to give him a good start to his life as the new Santa Claus. There is nothing like coming home to him, having him wrap his arms around me as we fall asleep, and seeing him by my side when I wake up in the morning.

And I'm still happy to massage his dick for him any time he needs it, whether he asks or not.

"Knock knock," a voice says from the doorway. "How's my operations manager handling her first Christmas on the job?"

"Is it always this stressful?" I ask, waving my hands over the mountain of broken toys on my desk. Each one is tagged with the name of the receiving child. Next to the toys is my laptop with an open spreadsheet on the screen. My days are nothing but spreadsheets now. Spreadsheets and conversations with my staff of elves, which is not where I saw myself in college.

Either I'm working on streamlining processes and writing procedures for Santa business, or I'm working on my own accounting side gig. Santa stuff keeps me busy from summer to Christmas, conveniently outside of high tax season. My January through May is all taxes now that I do other people's taxes under my own LLC. I thought it would be hard to find clients this year, but it turns out that Santa knows some pretty powerful people – people who can hurry through your LLC paperwork and recommend a few of their friends as clients. It's also helpful to know which IRS agents are naughty and which are nice.

Most of them have been very naughty.

Jasper crosses the room and cups my cheek. He's already in the Santa suit, and I have the sudden urge to unbuckle the huge belt buckle and peek down his trousers. He rubs my nose with his before placing a soft kiss on my lips. I wrap my arms around his neck and pull him closer, deepening the kiss and taking control of it. Even after eleven months of kissing and doing a lot more than kissing, I'll still drop whatever I'm doing for a little Jasper action.

He breaks the kiss. "This life is always stressful. Why do you think I visited a massage parlor last year?"

"Everything is ready to go on our end. There are a couple of toys being replaced, but you should have them within the hour." I salute him a little and step back.

"And the sorting system? You oversaw it, right?"

"Do you not trust anyone but me?"

He raises an eyebrow. "I only trust you. You should know that. I trust you with my life." His eyes darken as he says the last part.

"Everything is by geographical region now." I point at the air like I invented the lightbulb and turn to get a printout off my desk, showing him where he starts and stops during the delivery. "Drilling down further, you have it by state or territory, city, then quadrant, then it gets alphabetical. I also did a dry run on your GPS system. Just press the button, and you shouldn't need to touch it for the rest of the night. Your only job is controlling Prancer, which is a full-time job."

He nods and grins at me. "Did you miss that last part, Holly?"

"What last part?"

"That part about trusting you with my life. Because I do."

My stomach drops, and a blush creeps up my face. "What are you talking about? What's wrong?"

He drops to his knees in front of me. "I was going to do this after the delivery run, but I'm so nervous about it, I have to do it now or I'll...I'll have to go to a massage parlor to relieve stress or something. I won't be able to concentrate, and I'll have to pick up a hot masseuse to help me do the delivery." He chuckles, but I hear the nervousness in his voice.

"Jasper, are you...?"

He reaches into his suit and pulls out a black box. Opening it, I see his mother's ruby ring. I've seen it on her hand, and it takes me a moment to register that it's not on her finger any longer. It looks lost against the velvet in the box. Like it's without an owner.

"Is that your mother's ring?" I ask.

"With a twist. I changed the band out, resized it for you, and had two emeralds added here," he says, pointing to two small emeralds on either side of the circular ruby. "It's the Mrs. Claus ring. It's been worn by every Mrs. Claus in the family going back two-hundred years." He wipes a drop of sweat off his face as he explains. "Other Santas have added things to make it more modern. I wanted to make it different for you because you're different, Holly. You're so different from anyone I've ever met, and I can't imagine life without you. Will you be my wife?"

A tear spills down my cheek, and another drops onto Jasper's face. He doesn't wipe it away. He lets it slide off the side of his face as I stare into his eyes. Those eyes hold so much hope and love. Hope that I'll be his wife. Love that's unconditional. He doesn't care what I did for a job when I met him. He doesn't care about my flaws. He sees me as some type of goddess of female excellence and treats me like it every day.

If you had told me a year ago that I'd marry the guy that walked in for a standard massage and ended up enjoying a hand session, I'd have punched you in the face, especially if you told me that guy was the future Santa Claus.

He is Santa now. He's real, and he walked into my sad massage joint. I spit on his dick and jerked him off. I got in his sleigh that night and sorted his stock. I got him out of the police station when he was caught, and I played with the Tanners' sex toys with him and took a taser hit for him.

But I fell in love with the guy as soon as I saw him smile last Christmas Eve.

"Of course, I'll marry you, Jasper. Was there ever any doubt?"

He smiles his toothy grin, and his eyes crinkle at the corners. "I was a little worried. You've had a lot of life changes this year."

I pull him up by his shoulders, and he slides the ring onto my finger. I hold my hand up to the light, gazing at the ring on my hand, and let him cup my cheeks and stare at me. "We can get you something else if you prefer."

I shake my head. "No fucking way. I love it. Now that I know Santa and Mrs. Claus are real, I'm honored. I'm truly honored to be the next Mrs. Claus." I kiss him on the chin just below his mouth. "Do think that people will tell the story of a Mrs. Claus who gave hand jobs as her profession in a hundred years?"

"Oh, you'll be a legend, I'm sure," he chuckles. "Most Mrs. Claus predecessors knitted scarves or churned butter. My mother was the first that helped in the workshops and operations areas. You're also the first accountant Mrs. Claus and the first to have her own business on the side."

Our lips meet, and we kiss hungrily for minutes, my arms around his neck. His tongue mingles with mine as he runs his hands through my hair until we're both breathless. I glance at the desk behind us and then look at the clock. "Think we have time for a quickie, Santa?"

His pants drop to his ankles, and I grasp his cock as he lifts my green skirt, hooks his finger into my panties with little Christmas trees on them, and pulls the fabric down my legs in one movement. He lifts me onto the desk and nudges my legs apart.

This man is going to fuck me right on top of the delivery schedule spreadsheet printouts, and I couldn't care less that we may leave a wet spot on them so he'll have to decipher what the sheets say.

I pull away from our kiss and nuzzle his jaw. "One question," I say, running my hands down his cheek.

He raises an eyebrow. "Yes, you're on the nice list. It should have been naughty since you like to fuck Santa on your desk, but I'm in charge, so I do what I want. There are certain perks of being naughty when you're Santa's girl."

"Good to know, but that wasn't what I was going to ask."

He pushes his forehead against mine and closes his eyes as I wrap my legs around him, pulling him to me. "Will I have an answer?"

"You should," I laugh as he slides his dick home. "What's in the sack for the Tanners this year?"

THE END

Thank you for reading *All I Wank for Christmas*. Reviews and ratings are so important to indie authors, so please leave a rating or review on the platform of purchase. The more ratings and reviews indie authors have, the more readers we reach.

Want to know when I have a new release, freebies, or promos? Go to www.smuttybooklady.com and scroll to the bottom of the main page to sign up for my newsletter. If newsletters aren't your jam, you can follow me on Facebook or Instagram at @authortoriross. You can also catch my podcast *Sitting Here, Reading Corn with Tori Ross* on most major podcast streaming services.

What's next for me? *The Panty Plot* comes out in early 2024 and answers the eternal question of what happens when you sell your dirty panties on the Internet and your brother's best friend buys them.

Titles by Tori Ross-

The Cuffing Season Contract

Contact High

Rocks

Winning the Witch

The Flower Festival Fling

All I Wank for Christmas

The Panty Plot – Coming Soon

Disco Bar – Coming Soon

Hot Sauce Blues: A Short Romance

Head Over Heels in Hawaii

Loved in Las Vegas

Christmas on the Cruise Ship

Out of Luck in the Outback

Turkey in Tennessee

Acknowledgements

Whoo! I'm writing this after the book is completely done, and this is literally the last thing of the entire process. The relief I feel writing this can't even be explained, especially since I wrote this book in the middle of the hottest summer ever recorded and when my children were off from school. Do you have any idea how hard it is to write a Christmas book during a heat wave and when you're being relentlessly asked for corndogs or chicken nuggets?

But I got it done. Honestly, it was the people that preordered this that made this happen and kept me going. Thank you.

Thank you to my husband for letting me have the time to get this down on paper.

Thank you to my author friends: Evie Alexander, Kelly Kay, Selena Moore, Samantha Baca, and all the other mods over on the Cinnamon Roll Book Boyfriends Facebook group. I'd be in a ditch and crying without you. As it is, it's just the crying without the ditch. Thank you to Rachel Messerschmidt for the constant encouragement.

Thank you to my real-life friends: Lisa, Jaime, Chrissy, Paige, Bridget, Christie, the Vineyards ladies who asked about this story at the pool over the summer when I wanted to give up, and my ex-coworkers, Deb and Rebecca, for supporting me so much on social media. Actually, I receive a lot of support from my ex-coworkers. Since I once worked in education, this never ceases to amaze me.

Thank you to one of the many authors that wrote a book called "All I WanT for Christmas." There was one advertised last year where the "T" at the end of "Want" looked like a "K." I started laughing and then realized it really was a "T." The font was just weird. I thought to myself, "What a great name for a book." This is what resulted in that. Thanks for the writing prompt.

Lastly, thank you to my readers that fell in love with *Contact High* over on Kindle Vella and really kicked me in my ass to put more books out. I adore my readers...even the ones that give me shitty reviews. You took time to read something I created, and I can never thank you enough. Thank you for reading this!

About the Author

Tori Ross is the bestselling and award-winning author of steamy contemporary romance and romantic comedy. Her book, *The Cuffing Season Contract*, won the National Indie Excellence Award for romantic comedy, and she's written several shorts, novellas, full-length books and serials. When she's not writing, she runs a podcast called *Sitting Here Reading Corn with Tori Ross* and plays pickleball to get out of the house. She lives with her family and a hyper dog that needs extensive training.